The Steria

Nathalia Books

Published by Nathalia Publishing, 2021.

This is a work of fiction. Similarities to real people, places, or events are entirely coincidental.

THE STERIA

First edition. October 14, 2021.

ISBN: 979-8201178666

Written by Nathalia Books.

Table of Contents

Betray

Turnog

Standing on top of the lighthouse, Turnog looked out over the calm sea, the full moon shoveling twins into the waves. Soft and calming was the sound of waves crashing against the cliff face. He closed his eyes for a moment. It was cold that night, not colder than usual, but could feel it something was about to begin.

"Turnog?" He turned slowly, his sister standing behind him.

"What is it Ravana?" She walked over to him and stood next to him, she laid her hands on the railing and clinced them around the metal.

“There is nothing, really nothing. Even the residents of the Swawater keep quiet. ” He leaned back slightly and could see over her back the mountain group where the village of Swawater lay.

"Then what are you doing here?" Her eyebrows shot up and her back straightened.

"I wanted to know how you are doing, you are not the same since Isodora..." He raised his hand so that she had to stop. He really didný want to talk about that woman.

"PLEASE DON'T TALK TO me about that witch." She nodded with a sigh.

"No problem, I never liked her and I told you that several times." It was Turnog's turn to sigh and lowered his head, he knew she was right. She hadn't pushed her opinion under the couches and chairs.

"Is Sval in the tower?" She folded her arms and sighed, clearly noticing the change of subject.

"Where else should he be?" He shrugged for a moment. His gaze went to the wooden tower briefly illuminated by the lighthouse.

"I don't know, but I don't see any fire in the tower." He looked at her for a moment, her blond hair hanging loose on her back. One of her locks hung over her left eye, he always had a tendency to knock that lock away from there. But he also understood why that lock was hanging there.

"That is strange indeed." Her voice brought him back to the topic they were talking about.

"I'll go and have a look." She wanted to run away but he stopped her, by grabbing her arm as softly as posible.

"He's my best friend and you have to get back to your post at the Steria." She nodded for a moment, then looked back at the wooden tower.

TURNOG JOGGED DOWN the spiral staircase, the door leading to the adjoining house wide open. He walked through it without thinking, he didn't have to look back to know that his sister was falling behind him.

"Take my horse, it is already saddled." He looked back at her and gave a little nod.He strode out of the house, indeed there was his sister's black stalion. The animal was quietly nibbling on the tall grass that stood close to the stake to which it was tied. The animal noticed him and greeted him by stomping a few times on the dusty ground, a small cloud of dust surrounding it's hoof. He untied the animal and mounted with ease. For a pirate, then, he spurred the animal on and galloped through the moonlit night. The inhabitants of the houses of Truport, his port city since his father had brought him and his sister here, were in deep peace. The village trusted him to protect them as he had since his father was killed. The horse ran long into the tavern where light still shone behind the windows, the laughter and loud talk of the local drunks was clearly audible. He had a smile on his face, those were familiar sounds from Truport. But the sound faded into the still night as he drove on. The wooden watchtower was a now dark colossus, normally a torch burns in the top. That was not so much for sight as to let the people of the neighboring village in the mountains know that someone was watching them.

BUT NOW THERE WAS NO torch, strangely his best friend and First Mate Sval was normally a man of duty.

"Sval?" Turnog had arrived at the tower and was holding back the horse, the animal was a bit restless. He leaned forward slightly and stroked the animal's neck.

“Easy, boy. Calm down." But the animal began to buck and rear slightly. He jumped out of the saddle and tied the animal to one leg of the watchtower.

"Sval, are you there?" There was no answer and he was not sure if he had received an answer the first time.

"Sval, I'm coming up now!" He put his foot on the bottom step of the rope ladder.

"Turnog, sorry I fell asleep." Turnog frowned, there was something in Sval's voice that he didn't like.

"Fell asleep?"

"Yes!" torch started to burn, Turnog looked up and face Sval was visible. He could be wrong, but his friends face was a bit the red side. The shirt was also a bit messy, but that could be due to sleep.

"Well, sleeping beauty, during the time that you were sleeping. Could the gangs located in Swawater come across our bridge and attack. " Sval's face only turned redder, Turnog didn't trust it, and started the climb up. Sval turned redder and looked back quickly, now he was sure his friend was hiding something from him. He started to climb faster until his head came over the railing. He was standing on the ledge now, his eyes darting across the platform until he found what he was looking for. A woman was sleeping in a corner against the balustrade. The flames didn't reach far to reveal her face, but he could see the rest of her body. Turnog jumped over the railing and looked at his friend in amazement.

"WHAT DID I SAY ABOUT female company. It's fine, but not during your work, people depend on us. "

Turnog had his back to the woman and looked straight at his friend. Sval didn't look at him, but instead looked past him at the sleeping woman.

"Sval, what have you got to say for yourself?" He didn't know his friend in that way, especially when it comes to women. Turnog wanted to turn to see who had cast such a spell on his best friend, who must have been a very special woman.

"I'm sorry Turnog, it won't happen again. Promised. " His hackles rose, he got the feeling that Sval was not hiding the woman but who the woman was. As fast as he could, he turned and looked at the woman, who was now wide awake, staring at him with her sea-green eyes. He recognized those eyes out of thousands, his blood began to boil.

"In the name of the sea goddess Tishilla."

"Hey leave my mother out of this." The woman got up and her eyes flashed, but he didn't care.

"What are you doing here Isodora?" She turned, reached for her clothes, and without saying a word began to get dressed. He had completely forgotten about Sval, he only had eyes for her.

"Well what does it look like." She slowly lifted her dress and walked past him to Sval.

“Can you help me with my corset?” Sval just nodded and did what was asked of him. Turnog exhaled furiously.

“You know all too well what I mean, Isodora. Your pranks amost cost Ravana her live. "

Isodora shrugged indifferently.

"She survived, so don't worry." Turnog clenched his fists and stepped forward.

“How can I not worry, in which fantasy world do you live? You handed us over to Aqray's knot! ” Turnog looked away from her, his gaze went to the Steria that lay in the harbor. The three-master with her pristine white sails inherited from his father. '

"Did I hear that right, was the dragon of the sea afraid?" The mockery soaked her words.

"The Aqray’s knot is not a joke, it's just healthy to be afraid of the pirates hunters." She laughed and walked over to him and forced him to look back at her. Her face was close to his.

"I don't see any more of that fear now, you escaped that creep of a Summernight."

Turnog took her hand holding his chin and squeezed it hard, she hissed through her teeth with pain.

"That just didn't make much of a difference."

She began to laugh, once his heart melted at the sound. But now it only fueled his anger more.

"I forgot for a moment how serious you were, it almost hurts to see you like this." She turned to Sval, who visibly petrified.

"Fortunately you are not that boring." Giving Sval a kiss on the cheek, which couldn't get any redder. She pulled her lips off Sval's cheek and looked at Turnog. He took another step towards her and grabbed her by the arm. In his anger he squeezed a little harder than intended, for she let out a cry in pain. But he didn't pay her that much attention, he only had eyes for Sval.

"What did she promise you?" Sval looked down, unable to answer.

“Sval, what did she promise you? She promised you could become a captain. ” Sval still didn't answer him and this only made him more angry. Turnog let go of Isodora's arm, then grabbed Sval by the shirt.

"Then say something, man you stick a knife in my back and all I want to know is why." Isodora made a small noise that was much like laughter. But he didn't turn to her, his gaze sought that of his best friend. Who finally looked at him, there was something in Sval's gaze that terrified him.

"She has indeed promised me that, but that is not the reason why I did it." He looked at Sval not understanding, what more could he want. He could get gold and silver that way, no it had to be something he couldn't give him.

"HE WANTED ME, DRAGON of the sea." Said Isodora, in disbelief Turnog looked away from Sval and fixed his gaze on her.

"He can have any woman he wants, why would he want you?" She shrugged and now looked at Sval, too, who now took his hands and forced Turnog to let him go.

"Because I love her."

Anger gave way to disbelief, Sval had never shown any interest in Isodora. Sval had always followed Ravana like a shadow. Turnog slowly shook his head, even catching Sval sneaking out of Ravana's room several times. He was surprised he hadn't noticed the change in Sval's behavior. A slender hand fell to his shoulder, he looked at it and felt the rage rise again. Turnog pushed Sval, turned to face her. He grabbed her by the neck.

"Which spell have you cast on him!" She opened her mouth but couldn't answer. "Which spell."She took his hands and slowly turned blue. He let his grip weaken slightly, but still held her.

"You know all too well that I don't have a spell for love." Turnog cursed for a moment, but didn't let her go anyway.

"Turnog, let her go!" Sval's hands reached for his, one hand let go of her neck and gave Sval another hard push. But he kept looking at her, a loud scream was heard, then a cracking sound. Startled, he looked at where Sval had been, there was no one there now.

"NO!" TURNOG RAN TO the balustrade and looked over it, where Sval lay dead still on the ground. As fast as he could, he climbed down the rope ladder, knelt defeated. Sval's eyes and mouth were wide open, but his head was at an odd angle. A feminine cry filled the air, Isodora had also climbed down and stood sobbing behind him.

"You killed him!" He got up and shook his head.

"It was an accident." But she already raised her hands to the sky, every muscle in his body told him to get out of there. He took a few steps back, a ring of fire shot up, forming a barrier around her. He turned and ran to the now prancing gelding, as fast as he could, he untied the animal and climbed on its back.

ISODORA'S UNINTELLIGIBLE spell haunted him as he drove away from the watchtower. Turnog looked back in fear a few times, but she didn't chase him. Instead, a fierce wind rose, the world around him darkening. Thick dark clouds blocked the light of the moon, he urged the animal a few more times. He considered going back to the lighthouse, but he knew he would not be safe there from the wrath of Isodora. So he led the animal to the harbor where his ship Steria was, its hooves clattered on the wooden dock leading to the three-master. His gaze rose. Ravana was already standing by the gangway.

"Turnog, what's going on?"

"No time to explain. We have to go and quickly." He saw her look up as he dismounted and walked up the gangway.

"Is that Isodora the watchtower? Turnog where is Sval?" She took his arm, her white face told him she already knew the answer but she wanted to hear it out of his mouth.

"Sval had an affair with Isodora." The rest of the crew gathered around them.

"I caught them and with a little too hard push, Sval fell over the railing and broke his neck."

He looked at the faces of the crew looking anxiously at the clouds above their heads, Ravana took a step forward.

"It was not your fault Turnog, he betrayed us the moment he got involved with that witch. Now we have to get out of here! " To his surprise, she turned her attention to the crew and began to issue orders. The men spread across the ship and she took his arm. With little or no force she pulled him to the rudder, at the rudder she released him and grabbed hold of the wooden wheel.

"What are your orders, Captain?" He was still shaking a little, but started shouting orders.

"Hold on, this is going to be a bumpy ride." He moved closer to her.

THE WIND WAS NOW TUGGING at the white sails, the sea tossing them up and down.

"Looks like Tishilla agrees with her daughter!" One of the men ran to him with great difficulty. He looked at the man and cursed, he had hoped they were safe on the sea as this was the domain of the sea goddess Tishilla.

"Tell the men to constrict themselves, Riley!" He had to shout command to get above the wind and the sound of crashing waves. Riley nodded and ran away from him again with great difficulty. Ravana watched the sky as lightning shot from the dark clouds into the raging sea.

"If one of those bitches hits us, those safety lines won't help." He too looked up, a bolt of lightning came down and landed just next to the ship.

"I'm afraid that's the point." He walked over to her and put a hand on her shoulder, fear in her eyes. "I'm sorry." A bolt of lightning struck.

Arrival in Truport

Helana

The carriage drove through what her father called the sleepy harbor town, Helana knew better. The village had perhaps not changed in three centuries, except for the people who lived here. She looked at the white lime houses, she knew the village with the wind farms near the forest and the lighthouse on the cliff. Which came closer and closer.

"Helana, don't get stuck to the window like that." Her father's chastising tone did indeed make her look away from the surroundings and turn her attention to her parents opposite from her in the carriage.

"Come on dad, it's only summer once a year, which means we only come here once a year."

Her father sighed loudly.

"You are no longer a small child, next summer you will be part of the Aqray knot." She hung her head, how could she forget if he kept telling her. She closed her eyes for a moment and raised her head with a smile.

"All the more reason to enjoy it even more." Helena's gaze darted from her father to her mother, who visibly struggled to hold back her smile.

"Helana, please promise me that you will behave like a lady. Our family has been coming to this port city for three centuries and we have a reputation to uphold." She raised her shoulders.

"The people of this town have known me since I was a baby, they knew your father. We're no better than them, Aqray Knot is from this town." Her father took hold of her hand.

"That's because Captain Summernight's widow was not welcome anywhere else and the pirate who protected this town had disappeared too." Helana rolled her eyes indifferently, she had heard this story several times before, and she knew her father would quote it again.

The carriage came to a stop, her hand already reached the carriage door.

"HELANA." HELANA SHOCK from her fathers voice, she should have known this.

"I know father, first you then mother and then I will." He nodded in approval, but didn't look at her. When he opened the carriage door and jumped out. He helped her mother get out and, as usual, she romped with her way too long skirts. Helana had to go to great lengths not to burst out laughing, her mother looked at her for a moment and rolled her eyes. She knew that her mother, like her, cursed the long skirts and wished she was brave enough like her daughter to go against her husband to put on a short skirt. It was actually the skirt of her school uniform and it was indeed easier to get in and out of a carriage. Finally her mother had gotten out, the bottom of her skirt had a few streaks of dirt and dust.

"Now you can." Helana looked at her father with a narrowed look and then walked away from the carriage, she needed no help to get out. With ease she jumped out of the carriage and immediately walked over to the horses, which were panting in sweat. She patted both animals on the necks and reached into her small pouch that held two small apples.

"You spoil them, young lady." The driver came up to her.

"It's not a treat if the animals had worked for it." The driver nodded in agreement.

"Please help me with the suitcases, young lady, your mother has brought a lot of clothes for this trip." As he continued to discuss the amount of luggage women were taking, they walked around the carriage where the various suitcases were stacked. She wanted to pick up one of the suitcases.

"Helana!" Helana sighed if she couldn't help the driver with the suitcases. Something she did every year, she came up and turned her gaze to her father. Who stood with his arms folded in the doorway.

"Father, how can I ever run our family business if you deprive me of the simplest of tasks."

He shook his head.

"A lady those not carry suitcases!" Now she folded her arms.

"Something I have been doing since I was eight years old, in other words it is my responsibility and what do you always say about your responsibility!" Her father came to her with great strides.

"I said no." Helana leaned over to the first suitcase, which the driver had already taken off the carriage.

"And my job as a rebellious teenager is not to listen." She picked up the suitcase and walked past her father, her father took her by the arm.

"Put that suitcase down." She shook her head.

"Let her go Doc. She's right, she's been doing this for years." Her father looked up from her and looked at his wife.

"She's not a small child anymore, Liliana. It's time she adjusted to the norm." She ripped her arm free.

"I have been living by the norm all year round, at school and at home. But here, here I want to be myself." Helana walked to the door, her mother stepped aside.

"Doc, let her. The much you argue, the worse it gets."A sigh filled the air.

HELANA PUT HER SUITCASE in her own bedroom, turned around just as quickly. Everything was still in the place where she left it last year. The sailor cards were displayed on the wall. They hung there before she was assigned this room by her grandfather, who actually hoped that I would soon make room for a grandson. But when he came to the truth that her mother couldn't have any more children, it had become his life's mission to prepare her for the family business. Her father, who did not understand her behavior, never understood why his father gave her so much attention and taught her this behavior.She shouldn't think like a lady, she should think like a man. She went to the chest of drawers and opened the drawers to store her clothes she had brought.

"Helana?" She just closed her empty suitcase and came up, her mother was standing in her room.

"Have a little patience with your father, he doesn't think as freely as you and me." Helana shrugged, picked up her suitcase from her bed and slid it under the bed.

"It's called going with the times, mother, and not free thinking." She came up slowly.

"If he doesn't let me do anything out of the ordinary, how am I ever going to ..." Her mother raised her hand, which made her stop.

"Don't forget I'm on your side." She nodded and fell onto her bed with a sigh.

"I am sorry mother, but you know how it is." Her mother's answered a simple nod and then walked back to the door.

"Suzania has arrived and is waiting for you in the kitchen." Immediately she shot up, Suzania was the housekeeper and cook. Her mother's footsteps were already on the landing and down the stairs not much later.

"Suzania?" Helana walked into the kitchen with her head held high, a steaming cup of tea already waiting for her.

"Welcome back princess." Drunk with ridicule, Suzania walked into the kitchen.

"It's always an honor to come back, maiden Suzania from the land of Evergreen." They both laughed.

"Sit down and drink your tea, otherwise your father will think I'm putting you to work." Helana groaned softly.

"Please can't we talk about my father." Suzania nodded and sat at her kitchen table.

"So tell me, how was school?" She groaned again and told Suzania what had happened this year.

"I'M CALLED THE BLUE nun these days just because I focus on my studies and not boys."

Suzania laughed.

"There are worse nicknames." Suzania replied. Helana nodded reluctunted.

"I can't wait until next year, then I will finally be out of there and can take my place in the family business Aqray knot."

"What is this, are you galls chatting again?" A man entered the kitchen through the back door that led to the lighthouse.

"How nice to see you too, Mr. Treuman." The man shook a little with laughter.

"Ah, I thought I heard a familiar voice already." Her father also entered the kitchen and held out his hand to Mr. Treuman.

"How is she doing?" Treuman shrugged his shoulders slightly.

"I can't complain. She really is a Jewel of the sea." She looked at his face, it was clear he was avoiding something.

"Mr. Treuman, is something wrong?" He sighed, his gaze turned to her, and a thin smile appeared on his face.

"Nothing seems to escapes young lady." Helana sat a little straighter in her chair, the tone of his voice often not predicting good news. Her father had also noticed this and eagerly awaited the rest of the story. Mr. Treuman pointed to the chair, silently asking if he could sit down.

"Several fishermen have disappeared last year, more than usual. At first I didn't look for it, but then it happened every time around the full moon. "Her father sighed and shook his head.

"Come on Treuman, you know I don't believe in ghost stories." But she was already on the edge of her seat. Unlike her father, she loved ghost stories. It was a good picture of history.

"Was it the Steria?" Treuman nodded and turned his attention to her.

"You were always a quick learner, so I don't have to explain to you that the next full moon is tomorrow night." She turned her attention to her father, who shook his head in disbelief.

"DOC?" HER MOTHER HAD now also entered the kitchen, her father looked up at her.

"Come on Liliana, this is nothing more than a mere coincidence in combination with a sailor story." If she wasn't annyed with her father already, she would be.

"Maybe we should wait, father, until after the full moon. Not because of the sailor story."

She repeated his own words on purpose, letting him know she had listened to him. "But the moon makes the sea restless, extra high tides stronger storming."

Helana leaned back a little. "I know the Jewel of the sea is a strong boat, but we should not underestimate the power of the sea. Grandfather always told me that and I learned that at school this year too."

Her father frowend for a moment, but shook his head.

"Then make an extra offering to the sea goddess Tishilla, but we are going to sail tomorrow. Rain or shine, ghost ship or no ghost ship we are going to sail." Mr. Treuman got up form the wooden chair.

"Then I'll get her ready for departure." He left the kitchen with a heavy sigh and bowed head.

"I'll prepare your lunch and dinner. For the trip." Suzania also got up, now it was Helana's turn to get up.

"Then I'll go into town to get a sacrifice for the goddess, because I'd rather leave nothing to chance."

"You don't go into town alone." She turned, anger bubbled up inside her.

"Let me guess that is not the norm. Your father thought differently about that and I did too."

With those words she stormed out of the house and ran to the village.

HELANA DIDN'T STOP until she reached the first house, leaning forward to catch her breath.

"Hey Helana!" She came up a young man came up to her.

"Hey Valen, how are you?" She strode over to him and he shrugged.

"I am all right. Have you heard of the fishermen?" She gave him a small nod, his father is a fisherman by trade, just like his two older brothers.

"You're not going to tell me, are you?" He shook his head quickly.

"No, my mother does not want them to go out on the water with a full moon and as a good husband and sons they listen to her." He stood next to her and with a slight nod of his head they walked into town together.

"Unfortunately my father doesn't listen to his wife or me. So I get a sacrifice just to be on the safe side." Valen shook his head.

"It must be because he didn't grow up here." She nodded quickly, it probably would be.

"Then I can recommend the sea rose crown, my father says the sea goddess loves it." Helana frowned for a moment, then shrugged.

HELANA WAS STANDING on top of the cliff in her hands, holding the sea rose crown, a warm summer breeze playing with her hair.

"Sea Goddess, I hereby give you a rosary in the hope that you will take us in your arms." With a strong throw, she threw the wreath into the waves that gnawed gently at the edge of the cliff.

"Well spoken." She quickly turned to a strange woman standing behind her. "It just won't help you." A vague feeling of dread crept over Helana, the woman with her sea-green eyes that shone brightly. Helana straightened her back.

"What do you say that, can you see into the future?" The woman turned away from her.

"If you go sailing tomorrow, you and yours will not return."

Before she could respond, the woman had disappeared into thin air. Helana was still tongue-in-cheek to see where the woman who had just spoken to her had just stood.

"Who was she?"

"HELANA, DINNER IS READY!" Suzania's voice awakened her and she walked around the house, trembling slightly, to enter through the front door. "What's the matter with you, it looks like you've seen a ghost." Suzania stroked her hair gently, for a moment she considered keeping to herself what she had just seen. But Suzania's concerned look was so worried that she would do it anyway. After telling her story, Suzania gasped in alarm. "Isodora Lisica?" Suzania's gaze went straight to the portrait that hung in the dining room, her gaze went to it too. The portrait was of Captain Turnog, the last captain of the Steria. The lighthouse and the house on it belonged to the pirate captain before the captain's widow moved in. After what her grandfather had told her, the widow was so impressed with the pirate captain's accomplishments that she left everything the same and even left that portrait.

"Isodora Lisica, wasn't that the sea witch of the legend?" Suprise and fearful she suggested could only nod and demand Suzania.

"She's the one who cursed Turnog and his crew, I don't know about you but I'll do your best to convince your father not to go out to sea tomorrow."

Jewel of the sea

Helana

Helana sighed as Truport got smaller and smaller, they had left a little later than usual and that was her fault. But her father had persisted and now let's go, the sun was setting slowly and the full moon was beginning to climb.

"Helana, keep your eyes on the waves." Helana turned her head quickly, her hands clasped around the helm. She looked at the sail for a moment and it moved slightly to starboard and she turned the rudder a little bit. "Well done, Helana." It was a nice change to hear pride in his voice, in response she straightened her back and lifted her chin slightly in the air. Her mother's slender hand fell gently to her shoulder.

"It's great to be on the water again, it almost makes me forget what we talked about yesterday and this morning." The smile Helana had on her face immediately disappeared, Isodora's warning immediately surfaced. She shook her head to forget, her mother noticed the change in her attitude.

"I am sorry to bring it up." Helana shook her head again and steered the boat some more.

"It's okay, but I've always been taught to take all warnings to heart. Especially when the warnings are about the sea." Helana watched her mother's reaction with an oblique eye.

"Your grandfather taught you well, but he also taught your father and just like you now, he rebelled against his lessons." Helana looked at her father standing on the bow, he was not looking at them, but had his gaze on the sea.

"WOULD YOU LIKE A SANDWICH?" Her father was already approaching her with a sandwich in his hands.

"What's on it?" He raised his shoulders.

"I have no idea, but your name was on the paper. So I suspect something special." Helana let go of the helm with one hand and took the sandwich gently, there was a cooked egg on the sandwich. The moon was now at the top of the sky and the sun had sunk all the way into the sea, normally that would have been a disaster, but the moon was brighter than any other full moon she had seen. Her father came up next to her and looked at the moon.

"Do you know what that moon is called?" Helana kept looking at it, then closed her eyes.

"It's an Aqray moon because it's closer to the sea than usual." When she opened her eyes, he nodded approvingly.

"Who taught you that, your grandfather or those secret seafaring lessons." She gasped, a bit startled. She had enrolled in nautical classes at school, she was the only girl in the class. But the boys in her class, as well as her teachers, were surprised at what she already knew. But only Suzania knew that she was taking those lessons, how could he know. He started to laugh, probably one of her teachers had passed his mouth.

"I can explain." He shook his head.

"It's not necessary, your mother and I talked about it and she made me see that these lessons are good for you." Her jaw dropped. This was the first time he agreed with her, which was good for her.

"I got it from grandfather." His eyebrows came together slowly and wrinkles formed on his forehead. "I got the story from grandfather, it's said that Aqray god of the moon loved the Goddes of the sea. But when the mother of the goddes found out she banned him into the skies, only during the Aqray moon he is able to get so close to her." The wrinkles paused, but he nodded.

"FATHER, THE WIND IS picking up very fast." Helana felt she needed to tighten her grip on the helm, he ran to her.

"What do you suggest?" The bangs the sail made was deafening.

"Let we take down the sails before they tear." Her father looked at the sail and nodded.

"Liliana, let's lower the sail!" He ran to the bow to untie the rope, her mother ran to the sturgeon.

"Watch out mother, the sea is getting rougher!" That was to say the least, because the Jewel of the ocean was used as a rag ball that children threw on the beach. The tarpaulin came down slowly and the clapping stopped. But now the wind was howling in her ears, her father had a tight grip on the wooden railing. When he got close enough she could hear him.

"I'll take the helm!" She shook her head.

"I can do it, take you mother downstairs!" It was his to shook his head, her mother was right they where both staborn as hell.

"Don't think about it, I am your father." Anger bubbled in her. This was what she was trained for, did he forgot it already?

"This is not a debate, Father. I have the helm and that puts me in charge of this ship! Bring Mother below deck." His mouth fell open slowly, but he didn't argue. She tightened her grip on the helm as the heavens broke open. Many lightning bolts shot down, slowly lit the sea up. Although it gave an enchanting picture, she cursed it if she had done her best to convince her father to stay ashore for two more days. This was a very good replica of the great storm that sank the ship of her ancestor Captain Summernight and in which the pirate ship the Steria disappeared. She shook her head and prayed with all her heart to the sea goddess Tishilla.

"HELANA!" HER MOTHER'S voice rose dimly above the storm. Helana turned slightly and immediately cursed again. A three-master approached them, the white sails did not flap in the strong wind, but she fought the waves. The creaks of the wood repel the howl of the wind. Helana closed her eyes for a moment, but when she opened them, the ship was still there. A weird sea-green glow came from the ship's deck.

"Sailors story, yeah right!" Her father frowned for a moment, he had probably not seen the three-master yet. He was standing next to her now, supporting her mother. She gave him a little nod at the ship and he turned his head, a curse left his mouth. When he looked at her again, she saw fear in his blue eyes, his face was white too.

"I'm sorry, I should have listened to you." Helana nodded for a moment, tears running down her cheeks. She was afraid to look at her mother. A few masculine cries echoed through the night, the three-master now lying next to the Jewel of the sea. A whole group of men stood on the deck of the three-master, gasping for breath a few times to keep from screaming. The sea green glow came off the men and when she tried to look at the front line of men, but she couldn't see the faces. Helana wanted to let go of the helm and run. But if she let go, they would lose control and they would be completely lost. The first men jumped onto their decks and approached them with their weapons drawn. One of the men made it to her father, she cried out. While several men took the plunge, one of the men immediately approached her. Helana tried to look into his eyes, but couldn't see anything behind it. No eyelid and no iris, just a white void. The man raised his sword and slashed at her. She ducked down, the hair on her arms shooting up from the cold gust of wind. A female death cry rang and made her get up, looking around where the shout had come from. The group of men circled around something, again one cry rang to the air, this time a male. She bit her lip gently, tears now flowed. Something in her said she did not want to see what the men where hiding, but she wished that men step aside. Helana lowered her eyes and sobbed loudly, something that turned the pirates around. They had probably forgotten her, but their attention was back on her. Because when she opened her eyes, she felt a sharp point against the side of her neck. A man tugged at her arms that were still rusted around the helm. A painful sting gave way to the pressing sensation, and a warm liquid made its way down her neck.

HELANA FELT HER GRIP weaken just as the rest of her body slackened. With a final jerk her hands were pulled off the helm and she was carried away, half dazed she was pushed forward by someone. A wooden gangway had been laid out so that they could walk from one ship to another. She walked over it carefully, she had no energy left to fight back. But as soon as her feet touched the wooden deck, several pains shot through her. Her legs started to give way, but someone held her up.

"Take this landlubber to gibbet." Helana was pushed into someone's arms, there was no answer, but no doubt she was almost lifted.

"Where do you think you're going, Glam." The person who lifted her stopped when she heard the woman's voice.

"I had to take her from Skegg to the gibbet." She could not see what was happening, but the man let her lose. She landed on the wooden deck with a thud, feeling her consciousness slip away. She was grabbed by the chin and jerked to look into someone's eyes. This time the eyes had no white features but there was one light brown and the other sea green.

"Why did you take her?" The question sounded like a whip.

"She has a strong soul, Ravana. Skegg had to injure her to get her hands off the helm." Ravana's eyebrows shot up.

"How many men?"

"Skegg, Morgan and myself." She whistled slightly.

"A strong soul indeed. But the outside." Ravana shook her head and let her go. Her head fell again on the wooden deck.

"Take her to my room, which is more suitable for a woman." Helana was jerked to her feet.

"Do you think it's her?" Ravana shrugged indifferently, shook her head for a moment, leaving a tuft over her sea-green eye.

"No idea, time will tell."

HELANA WAS THROWN ONTO a thin mattress.

"Here we are princess." He walked away with big dull thumps and with a bang the door was slammed in the lock. Her body was shaking with fear and pain, she tried to get up for a moment, but her arms actually gave up immediately. She closed her eyes, the image of her parents covered in blood on the deck of the Jewel shot up instantly. Again she felt tears sting behind her eyes. "We're not whining here on board." Her eyes shot open and with her last bit of strength she pushed her head slightly upward. An obese man stood in front of the closed door, quickly swallowing her tears.

"I'm sorry about your parents princess, your father was a brave man." Helana lowered her head, who was that man and why did he look different from before.

"Brave or not, it failed to save its life." The man started to laugh, it seemed as if the room was shaking slightly at the sound.

"Spoken like a true pirate, princess." She frowned for a moment.

"Why do you call me princess?" The man laughed again, she did not chaught the joke.

"It is just a nickname until I know your real name, princess" She rolled her eyes she should have known it was such a simple thing. "How do you feel now." Helana frowned for a moment before entering this conversation, feeling lifeless. But now she felt better, even the cutting pain she had experienced had gone. She pushed herself up.

"Physically good, but mentally" He nodded and folded his arms.

"Try to forgive us, princess. We weren't ourselves. But now that you're feeling better I'll take you back to the deck." She got up slowly from the bed, he gave her a smile, beckoning her with his head.

"Helana." He turned around in surprise.

"Sorry?"

"My name is Helana."

THE SUN CARESSED HER face, the salty sea breeze blew through her hair. tilted her head a little, it was night less than a few hours and judging by the sun it was now the middle of the day.

"Did I sleep?" The man laughed.

"No, princess. We're just somewhere we weren't just before." She wanted to ask further, but he grabbed her arm.

"Stay close to me, the captain is not that friendly and the first mate you have already met."

She nodded for a moment, then bit her lip.

"She doesn't really like me and I can't blame her." A seagull flew over the ship, the animal's cries scaling through the air. Helana walked to the edge of the deck and turned her gaze to the harbor town that was getting closer and closer. The white lime houses seemed vaguely familiar to her, when she saw the lighthouse she was sure. They sailed towards Truport, she looked at the pirate next to her. Who saw her surprised face.

"Aye, our home."

"But you just said we were somewhere different from where we just were." He nodded.

"We are in a different realm." Helana turned and her mouth fell open, behind her was Captain Turnog.

Knot Unravels

Turnog

Her brown hair, flapping carelessly in the wind, was the first thing he noticed. Her stately attitude, yet strange costume. She wore nothing more than a blouse and a simple but short skirt. Turnog stared at her for a moment.

"That's the girl from that one-master. According to Skegg she has a strong soul, I just don't see it." Ravana was standing next to him, he just shrugged.

"All I know is that her ship had the The Aqray's knot on it's color, only this one had another color. " Her eyes widened in surprise.

"You think she knows more about Captain Summernight? The others didn't even know who he was." A low growl left his throat and she immediately raised her hands.

"Sorry to bring it up." He returned his gaze to the young woman standing on the deck of his ship. Skegg was standing next to her.

"I'm just going to introduce myself, as befits a good host." Turnog heard her sarcastic hiss and was almost certain she rolled her eyes. As a captain, he should actually correct her, but since she was his sister too. He straightened his back slightly and walked past the various crew members, each greeting him and nodding his head politely at them. He was lucky to have such a good crew, even after what happened to Sval. Everyone actually agreed with Ravana, he betrayed us, so it was his own fault. But even after they were cursed into this realm, where none of them grew up and was forced to stay. He shook his head for a moment, now standing behind the young woman and Skegg who had already seen him.

SHE ONLY HAD EYES FOR Truport and was probably amazed at the change of time. She asked Skegg a question, but Skegg looked at him

"We are in a different realm." Immediately she turned, a surprised look met him. Turnog didn't have to introduce himself like that, her lips formed his name. Now it was his turn to be amazed, the other women who had followed them to this realm had not known who he was and had quickly wanted to leave when they found out he was a pirate.

"This is our Captain Helana, Turnog." Skegg had broken the silence as he always does, Helen bowed her head slightly.

"It is an honor to meet you the legendary Captain Turnog." Turnog opened his mouth, but words failed him. She called him legendary, that was something new.

"But what's your name, princess." Ravana had seemingly followed him, and her sharp tone of suspicion was evident, as always with strangers. Helana had apparently noticed, too, and raised her chin a little more.

"My name is Helana Summernight, my ancestor was Captain Summernight." There was a gasp around him, he raised his hand.

"Ancestor, how many years has it been after Array's departure?" Helana looked straight at him.

"You disappeared in the year 700 and you were just in the year 1000."

"She lies!" Ravana stepped forward, grabbed Helana's arm and pulled her towards her.

With a simple movement, Helana pulled herself free.

"Why should I lie, tell me." Helana's blue eyes fired with rage, Ravana looked at him expecting to intervene. Turnog folded his arms, this was her own fight and he didn't want to get involved. Ravana therefore looked at Helana again.

"If what you say is true, we have been dead for 300 years." Helana shrugged for a moment, Ravana walked away with a cry of frustration.

"Forgive my sister, she's a different type." Helana shrugged again.

"I get it, I'm the intruder here." Turnog nodded, she not only had a strong soul, but also a good brain. Turnog knew he had to watch out, but something in him was starting to like her.

"CAPTAIN, WE ARE SAFELY at ports." Turnog motioned for her to come along, but she stayed where she was.

"Aren't you coming?" Helana shook her head.

"Why should I trust you and especially you, it was your men who killed my parents. Kidnapped me from my realm." Her voice was soft, but he was sure the crew already around them had heard her. Skegg stepped forward.

"We weren't ourselves." Helana did not let her gaze wander from him, the same fire of anger still burning. But her anger was directed at him this time.

"I've heard this excuse before, but what drives someone to kill innocent unarmed people.

She might have been smart and indeed had a strong spirit, but now he could add courage too. Only now she was too brave for the position she was in. Skegg sighed for a moment and picked up Helana, uttering a little cry of shock and frustration. With tremendous simplicity, Skegg threw her over his shoulder and walked down the walkway with Helana protesting heavily.

WITH A SMILE ON HIS face, heard her slapping and kicking at her bedroom door, several screams mingled in the sound.

"I can silence her." Ravana had her gutter, a wooden stick with a sharp point at the end, in her hands.

"So you're not going to do that, she's here against her will. We killed her parents and now she's stuck with us. What you're going to do is go to your clothes box and find some more suitable clothes for her. Those rags might be just for her time, in our time. " Turnog had to duck and the gutter landed in the wall behind him.

"I don't trust her, she's a Summernight." He nodded and he knew his sister all too well, this was the point where she brought in Isodora.

"I was right about Isodora and I dare to put my soul to it that I am right about her."

Bingo there she was, every time she brought up Isodora.

"Let her rest, before all we know, Isodora is long dead." Ravana sighed and looked at him.

"If you want to believe that, I'll leave it that way. But if we're here what would stop her to come as well." Turnog hit the table with his fist.

"Let her rest, I'm not going to repeat myself a third time." Ravana took his clenched fist with her hands.

"I will do what you ask me to do, but I will not stop expressing my opinion." Ravana let go of his hand and left the room.

TURNOG SAT ALONE IN the dining room, the smell of roast meat and baked bread filling the room. His stomach began to growl. How could he be hungry, he had had a hearty breakfast before they left for the other realm. But every time he bumped into the same problem, while Skegg was busy in the kitchen he could wander in his mind. But no matter how he tried, his mind kept drifting to the young woman who was in his house at the moment. Her brown hair and her blue eyes where behind a cesspool of emotion. Turnog wasn't quite sure if he should keep his distance, or. He shook his head, his mind was playing tricks on him again. This was only temporary, it always was temporary.

"Captain?" Skegg entered the room, holding the fresh bread.

"What is it?" Skegg put the bread on the table and his head slowly turned red. Skegg was never shy so what changed.

"Shall I send a bunch of sea roses for your guest?" Tunrog frowned slightly, it was a good idea. In this way he was able to express his regret for the death of her parents and it brightened up her temporary shelter for a while.

"Go ahead and throw a rosecrown off the cliff too. To thank the sea goddess." The stout cook nodded a moment, then walked back to the kitchen to get the meat.

HELANA ENTERED THE dining room, Ravana behind her. The same fire of determination still burns in her eyes. She was now wearing a long light blue dress that matched her eyes.

"Sit down, you must be hungry?" Turnog gestured to the chair across from him and she sat down without protesting, but she kept looking at him.

"We are going to eat first and then I have some questions for you." She shrugged her shoulders.

"Well, that's a good thing I also have some questions for you." A crooked smile appeared on his face and he could only nod, this was the fire he had seen on the Steria before. A thought occurred to him, but quickly suppressed these thoughts. She was here, but temporary, and he couldn't bear to burn his fingers on the fire, however sweet the wounds might be. His gaze went to his sister who gave him a penetrating look, the same warning was in her gaze. He took the bowl of meat and put some meat on his plate.

"I hope you like beef because that's all we have. Until we rob a new freighter, of course." His gaze was on his plate, but when he got no answer, he looked up anyway. She just put a piece of meat in her mouth and chewed it lightly, she had been raised as a lady somewhere he could have expected. Though perhaps her costume confused him. Ravana cleared her throat and it caught his attention, looking at him accusingly. He knew what it meant and he was not happy about it.

SKEGG ENTERED THE DINING room and cleared the dishes.

"Shouldn't you eat?" The concern in Helana's voice was evident, Skegg laughed but his face turned slowly red.

"Don't worry princess, me and the men are eating in the tavern." Skegg walked back to the kitchen with his hands full. Ravana got up from the table and picked up the things Skegg had left behind.

"I'll help him with the dishes." Those were Ravana's words before she disappeared into the kitchen, now he was alone with her. Helana looked at him now, was not surprised.

"Well Helana Summernight, I would like some more information about your ancestor." She nodded and put her clasped hands on the table.

"What do you want to know?" She was sharp, there was probably a knife from the evening meal on her lap. He decided to ignore it for a moment before Ravana burst into the dining room again and took the knife from Helana.

"Preferably everything." Helana nodded and touched her mouth with her tongue.

"Well, as far as I know, he was killed in the great storm. The same storm in which the Steria disappeared, but his ship was found later. According to the stories, he was waiting for you until you chose the open water, because according to the law of the land he could not touch you here. But on the open sea. " He nodded, he knew the rules of the country, he was safe here. But he was an outlaw on the open sea.

"Is it wrong to say I'm glad he got the sailor grave?" Helana rolled her eyes for a moment.

"His widow would not agree with you, she was left with three children and had nothing. She was forced to leave her city and country. She came to the only place on earth where she knew everyone was welcome, including a pirate. " Turnog frowned and went through all the places he knew, but he didn't have to think hard about it. Truport had always opened his arms to those who needed help, which he was very proud of.

"But no matter how much Truport's people helped her, she was a proud woman. She and her eldest son therefore founded a trading company and that company still exists today. She started that company from this room." He stiffened for a moment, the people of Truport had given Summernight's widow his home. Helana had probably seen the tightening in his position and a smile appeared on her face.

"SHE MIGHT NOT HAVE a penny to her name, but she heared such beautiful stories from the people of Truport that she had kept everything the same in the house. Even your portrait is still there."

Helana pointed to the goatskin cloth that Ravana had painted. So she knew him from that, not only from stories but also from sight. Turnog swallowed, clearly impressed by the story.

"Your ship had Aqray's knot as its symbol." Helana gave him a single nod.

"The knot of Aqray, went down with my ancestor. His widow simply used the symbol and gave it a different color, also called her company Aqray's knot."

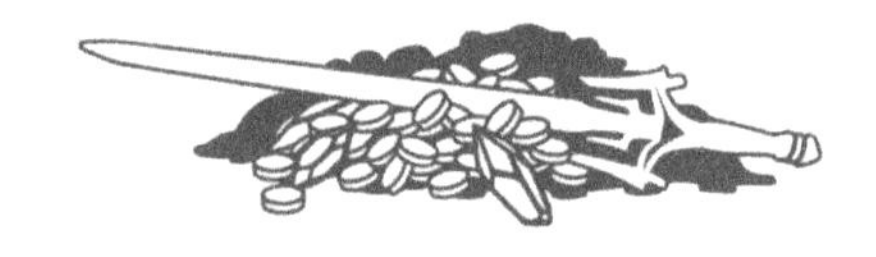

AS PREDICTED, RAVANA burst into the dining room, holding her gutter in her hand.

"Helana, why don't you give that knife to my sister." S he looked at him in surprise and he loved the expression on her face, with visible reluctance she handed the carving knife to Ravana. Who had also looked at him in surprise for a moment, but when it touched her hand, she disappeared back into the kitchen.

She

Turnog

The salty sea breeze blew through his dark red hair, the scar on his left cheek stung a little. It was something that happened more and more often, Turnog didn't normally spend time and attention on it. But it started to hurt more and more, his right hand went to the cheek.

"Those it sting again?" Ravana stepped up to him, pinning her gaze to the horizon where the sun was slowly sinking into the sea.

"Why do you ask that, does your scar also sting?" He looked at her from the corner of his eye, her hand went to her neck where her scar was.

"It gets worse every time we go to that other realm and come back after that." He nodded for a moment, but did not go into further detail.

"You have to watch out, brother." Turnog sighed, there was his big sister again.

"I know you're right, but she looks so much like someone, but unfortunately I don't who."

Ravana turned to him and sighed."That's because you were too young, but her whole character resembles mother's character." The sun disappeared into the sea, he frowned. He hadn't thought about his mother for a long time. He couldn't even envision her face, his father had said several times that Ravana looked a lot like her in her appearance then. Now he thought about it, he had not thought of his father recently.

"Do you remember her?" Ravana exhaled with a bated breath and folded her arms.

"I have to say, I haven't thought about her for a long time." He nodded for a moment.

"The same here." Ravana gave him a smile, the first moonlight lit her face. The tuft of hair that normally covered her sea-green eye blew away.

"WHAT I REMEMBER IS that I often had to look after you when she had a male guest again. But always before a guest came we got a piece of fruit or something sweet." She looked to the ground.

"What always stayed with me was the day that father came to pick you up. Mother kept begging him to take me too, but he really didn't want it. At first I didn't want to come either. But mother had asked me to watching you, I knew she was sick. I just didn't know how bad it was. "

A tear shimmer in the moonlight. "The day father you wanted to take, and he wanted to see her, he had asked me to go get her. I run towards her bedroom, something in me stopped me to push the door open. However, at knowing better, I still opened her room door and she was no longer there. "

Another tear glittered in the moonlight, he knew this was a difficult subject for her.

"You don't have to tell if you don't want to." Ravana shook her head and sighed.

"That's not the problem. You need to know this and there's no one else to tell you. So when I found mom, I ran to dad. I didn't say a word, but he probably saw it in my face. He stormed into mother's room, along with her pimp. I heard the pimp talking to him and when he came back he took us both. On the Steria he encountered some negative ones from the crew. " Turnog nodded, he knew what those negative reactions were. He too had received these reactions when he took Ravana on board for the first time.

"A woman brings bad luck." Turnog had only laughed at that stupid superstition, he had never been so lucky since Ravana came on board.

"But when we got here and he started training you, I was allowed to watch."

"Would you also like to participate?"

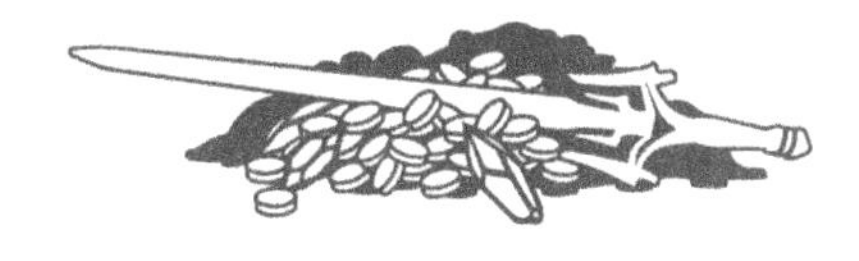

THEY BOTH TURNED AROUND, Helana was behind them. She was holding a single sea rose in her hand.

"Sorry, I didn't want to bug you. But I always came here when I needed to think." Turnog looked in surprise at Ravana, who shrugged.

"No I was not allowed to train, but I trained in secret. Until my father caught me, I remember standing at the edge of the practice field, he did nothing but look. Until I noticed him and then he came to to me. With these in his hands. " Ravana pulled her gutter from her belt, the weapon circling between her hands for a moment. "From that moment on, we trained every day to master it." Helana nodded and gave Ravana a smile.

"It's a beautiful weapon, it can be used by stabbing and throwing." Ravana's eyebrows shot up and nodded approvingly.

"Someone has your well-educated princess." Helana shrugged, took a few more steps forward, and threw the rose into the sea.

"We will see each other again." Turnog lowered his head a little.

"Very well trained." Ravana's voice rose slowly, and he knew she was impressed.

"My grandfather taught me a lot and everything I didn't know I learned in school." Turnog repeated the word school in his head, frowning for a moment.

"What is school?" Helana began to giggle softly, but continued to gaze at the Black Sea that captured a copy of the full moon.

"Do you mind if I tell you tomorrow, because to be honest I don't know how to explain it."

Turnog nodded for a moment and continued to listen to the waves crashing against the cliff.

THE THREE OF THEM STAND for a moment, he enjoyed the silence. Ravana was the first to leave the group, but not much later Helana went to her room, which he had given her. Turnog just stood there for a while, she came here to remember her parents and she spoke the sacred words. He shook his head, every time he saw her, he discovered something new.

"She's far out of your reach, Captain." His neck hairs rose, that voice. He had hoped never to hear it again.

"What are you doing here, in my personal underworld that you created especially for my friends and me?" The invisble woman sighed and came to stand next to him.

"You also know this was not meant to be, was meant to kill you. Not knowing that magic had any more limits." He growled softly.

"You are trying to avoid the question, what are you doing here Isodora?"

Isodora started to laugh.

"I live here, Turnog. Just like you, I am trapped here until that curse is broken. But unlike you, I live on." He frowned for a moment, he wanted to ask further but swallowed his question. She didn't go through with it either so it was something he would find out once the curse was broken, if it meant that he and his men were going to die at least they would finally find peace. However, he felt more guilty, because that would mean that he killed not only Sval that day but the rest of his crew as well.

"I'll leave you alone with your thoughts, Captain. But I'm sure we'll resume this conversation before the third full moon appears in the sky." Isodora seemed to disappear into thin air and he was alone again.

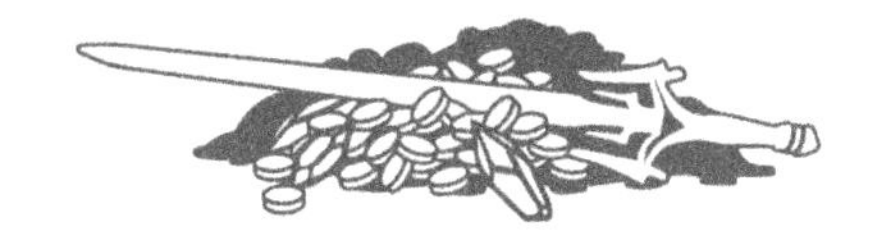

TURNOG CONSIDERED GOING inside for a moment, as he knew himself and knew the thoughts would keep him awake. Still, against his better judgment, he walked in, but walked through the kitchen to the spiral staircases that lead to the lighthouse. He started the ascent to the lamp room, where the large fire pit was already burning thanks to Skegg. He sat down by the firepit.

"Can't sleep?" Skegg came up with heavy footsteps, but the surprise on his face told him more than the question he had just asked. Turnog nodded for a moment, then looked back into the firepit.

"Tomorrow we have to clean the mirror and grease the wheel." All Skegg could do was nod, it was the normal duties he and the rest of the crew had when they were ashore. Skegg sat down next to him and let out a deep breath.

"I confess captain, Helana is the first woman we have taken that I really like." His eyebrows lifted slowly, Skegg was not the person to make his feelings heard. Something he appreciated, especially when it had to do with people outside the crew. Even when Isodora betrayed them he had kept his opinion to himself, and even when Sval betrayed them by getting involved with Isodora, he was the only one who did not speak up about the situation.

"I know what you mean, but we shouldn't get attached to her." Another heavy sigh came from the sturdy pirate.

"I know Captain. But what if she's the one who can break the curse." Turnog nodded.

"Then again Skegg, we don't know what breaking the curse is. But knowing the silver fox it can't be a good thing." He hardly ever used Isodora's nickname, even when Sval came up with that nickname. Just like its own nickname the dragon of the sea. He heard Sval say it.

"Pirates need a cool nickname."

"Whatever the silver fox may have planned, we must not forget to enjoy the time we have."

Turnog closed his eyes for a moment and sighed, this was another thing that will probably haunt his mind all day tomorrow.

"CAPTAIN?" A HEAVY HAND landed on his shoulder and shook him gently from side to side. Turnog slowly opened his eyes, the early sunlight making it's way through the windows. "I'm sorry Captain, I couldn't bring myself to wake you sooner." He stretched for a moment and gave the sturdy pirate a smile.

"Doesn't matter, it was nice to get some sleep. Something I didn't expect." Skegg laughed.

"That was always something your father said when I was still serving under him." The smiles immediately turn into a grimace. That happened every time he was compared to his father, he got up and stretched again.

"Give the jobs to someone else and lie down for yourself, you've earned it." He patted Skegg on the shoulder.

"If you're looking for me I'll be in the stables." He went downstairs and didn't look up or around as he walked through the kitchen.

"GOOD MORNING," TURNOG froze before walking through the door to the rest of the house. Helana was standing by the stove, only now did he notice the smell of onions and eggs.

"Good morning too, you're up early." She shrugged her shoulders.

"I couldn't sleep, so when the sun came up I got up." He looked a little worried, she couldn't sleep either, maybe the room wasn't good.

"My room was fine, to be honest it's the same room my grandfather gave me. The only difference is there are maps in it." Turnog gasped, how could she know he was wondering. Helana kept staring at him, was it a good guess or was she some other sea witch who just happened to read minds.

INSTEAD OF GOING TO the stables, Turnog sat down at the kitchen table and watched her cook breakfast. Ravana entered the kitchen not much later.

"Good morning little brother and princess, where's Skegg?"

"I gave him the morning off." Ravana's eyebrows shot up, amazed that he could still amaze her after all these years together. "He was up all night and he's not the youngest anymore."

Ravana sat down next to him so she could listen to him and most likely keep an eye on Helana.

"You're right about that, he was already working for father when he picked us up."

Helana put two mugs of a steaming liquid in front of their noses, a little awkwardly he grabbed the stone mug and brought it to his mouth.

"Wait a minute, it's still hot." But her warning came too late, he had already burned his mouth. But he tasted the slightly salty stuff, it was tea.

"Which goods ship did you have to rob for this" It made her laugh, the sound enchanted him.

"This is sea rose tea and I made it myself."Ravana slapped the table with a flat hand.

"Homemade, you don't make your own tea unless you are a witch."

Helana shrugged and continued frying the eggs.

"You asked me what school was yesterday, I've been thinking about that all night and I think I have an answer." Helana slid the eggs one by one from the bronze pans onto the china plate. "It's an institution where a group of experienced adults, teaches the younger generation important skills they may need itn life. It's just like your father did with you, but with larger groups." Turnog nodded for a moment.

"Did you learn to make tea at that school?" It was her turn to nod.

"Sea rose tea is good for renewing energy." He took another sip of the sea rose tea and he could imagine it. In this way the knowledge was transferred more easily, especially if they were allowed to choose which knowledge they acquired. Ravana was also deep in thought as she sipped the tea.

HELANA LEFT THE KITCHEN for a moment and Ravana leaned over to him.

"No wonder she's so smart, she not only had her grandfather, but also that school,who taught her several things." Turnog nodded.

"But I see the point in it, if such a thing existed, father could send us there and he could sail himself." Ravana hissed and shook her head.

"He would send you there and what he would do to me, no idea." Ravana sat down normally again, he had to agree with her with a smile on his face. Father was a nice man to him, but when it came to Ravana, his father was tougher and set higher standards.

"He loved you, I'm sure." She got up and collected the empty plates.

"I'll never know if you're right."

What makes sense?

Helana

The voices of Ravana and Turnog came through the door. It was very difficult not to look at Ravana with different eyes, Helana had not had an already good relationship with her father, but Helana knew that her father loved her. They kept talking and she didn't want to disturb them again in a private conversation, she turned away from the door and walked out the front door. Seagulls argued in the air, the waves crashed against the cliff. She took a deep breath, a horse neighed in the distance. She walked back to the cliff where the salty wind began to play with her hair. This was paradise, she sighed and closed her eyes. An image of Turnog's face appeared instantly, she frowned and shook her head. What was he doing in her mind, he was 300 years older than she was. Helana rolled her eyes while they were still closed, that was actually the first argument she could come up with. Not that he was responsible for the murder of her parent, he was the one who took her to this prison. But no he was too old, of all the things she had heard from legends it was always the younger woman who fell for the older man and actually she had always mistaken those women for stupid. But that she was in a legend herself.

"Difficult thoughts?" Ravana had come up next to her, she opened her eyes and nodded a little.

"I have a weird feeling that I'm going to make the biggest mistake of my life."Ravana nodded and folded her arms. For a moment they watched the sea-green sea together, listening to the waves and the seagulls still arguing in the sky.

"Maybe it's a good idea to listen to your feelings." To be honest, she was not surprised that Ravana said this to her.

"I understand why you want me away from your brother, I can't say I'm speaking from experience." Ravana turned to her.

"You think you understand, but you never fully understand."

"I understand you don't like me." Ravana closed her eyes and shook her head.

"I really like you, even though I don't really know you. You have something about you that reassures me, it's just that too many women hurt him and because of that I don't trust any other woman around him. Also the one who I did not trust Isodora and to be honest I curse myself for being right. " Helana nodded for a moment, she didn't even know what she was feeling, it could just be admiration.

"I would never want to hurt anyone intentionally, hopefully you feel that way too."

Ravana nodded and reached out to Helana, who grabbed Ravana's hand.

THEY WERE JUST OUTSIDE the stables, a black gelding stood between them.Helana brushed the loose hair and dust off the animal's skin.

"What a beautiful animal." Helana patted the animal on the neck, the animal hung its head for a moment and blew loudly into the small clod of grass beneath it.

"Did you hear that Thunder, you are a beautiful animal." Thunder blew the grass again, both women burst out laughing.

"What's so funny?" Turnog came out of the stable with a soft brown mare. Helana almost dropped the brush from her hands, the animal looked so much like the horse her grandfather had.

"Helana?" She realized she'd been staring, probably with her mouth open.

"Sorry my grandfather's only interest other than training me was horses and one of his last looks exactly like yours?" He looked at his horse and brushed it over its neck.

"Well, Helana, this is Inco."

The animal reared for a moment when he mentioned her name, then it bent one of its front legs and knelt before her. She almost got tears in her eyes, because it was beautiful to see that the animal had so much faith in the people around her.

"So you can drive too?" Helana shook her head.

"No my grandfather died before he could teach me and if I had asked my father I would have killed him in your place. Certainly because then I would not behave like a lady of class, but like a boy who grandfather liked to. " She could sigh Ravana behind her.

"Are all fathers the same in there?"Helana gave her a smile and shook her head.

"I don't believe that, some of the girls in my class have a bit more freedom. But my grandfather just wanted a grandson to take over the business, but when he was told that no grandson could come, he devoted all his attention. to me and my training. He just taught me to think like a man in a woman's body and I have to be honest since those lessons I was not the easiest for my father. " Turnog nodded for a moment, meanwhile he had taken a stiff brush and now he started brushing with hard long strokes

"But at least you have learned to think for yourself and that is a good quality." Her cheeks were burning something she hadn't expected, her hands quickly went to them.

"I'm going to have a drink, excuse me."

IN THE KITCHEN HELANA leaned forward for a moment to catch her breath, when she was out of sight she had started running. If she had blushed closely, she had never seen it before and certainly not near a man.

"Helana?" There he was again, she quickly came up and walked to the counter. Where she was looking for a crane, she had it in her relam, but where was it here. "What are you looking for?"

Helana turned to him, he leaned against the door frame.

"You certainly don't have a tap for clean water." Turnog shook his head.

"I don't even know what a tap is, but if, as you just described, it ensures that we can get clean water into the house. Without any of us having to walk outside to the well, that's a good invention." She sighed and put both hands on the counter.

"Where's that well?" Turog gave her a smile, she felt her cheeks glow again. "Are you okay?" Helana nodded for a moment, then turned quickly so that he could no longer see her face. His boots made a heavy noise that came closer and closer, suddenly a big rough hand landed on her shoulder. A little cry left her throat, he started to laugh.

"I'm sorry I scared you, but I have some water here." She started to laugh with him, but it was difficult to keep her hands still. She put the nearly empty stone mug to her mouth and drank the last sip of water.

NEVER BEFORE HAD HELANA been so embarrassed, he had watched as she nearly choked on that little bit of water. She was now in a chair, his hand running slowly across her back, something inside her screaming that he shouldn't stop. But she narrowed her eyes and got up again.

"I'm fine." Helana could read the concern in his eyes.

"Are you sure?" She nodded and brushed her long hair back with both hands. She strode out of the kitchen and out through the rest of the house. She never looked back, but she was sure he was following her.

"Really I am fine." She turned and looked straight at him, worry had given way to twinkles and a big smile. She wasn't sure whether to smile back or slap him in the face with a flat hand.

"Captain, Captain!" Helana turned to see Skegg running up the hill with great difficulty. She took a big step aside, as far as her dress would allow. She really had to ask Ravana for pants, they would make moving a lot easier.

"What's the matter Skegg?" Turnog walked out of the house, Ravana also came running. The man's face was bright red and could barely speak for lack of breath.

"I'm going to get him some water!" She was about to run, but then saw a woman standing behind the man's back. Her blood froze, that was the woman she'd seen in her realm. Suzania had named her Isodora. Inadvertently she moved closer to Turnog and even though she wouldn't admit it, the woman scared her.

"TURNOG." RAVANA HAD also noticed the woman, a hand fell on her arm and that reassured her a little.

"Get away Isodora, you are not welcome here!" The woman shrugged but did not walk away. Instead, she came closer.

"That's not what you said yesterday." Her voice flowed over her like a cold shower, it slightly tightened the grip on her arm, so they had already seen each other last night.

"He may not, but I'm telling you silver fox now. You're not welcome here." Ravana took a step forward and Isodora looked offended but now stopped.

"Such harsh words, but luckily I am not coming for you. I am coming for the girl." Isodora's finger jabbed at her, she swallowed visibly. As with her feelings for Turnog, she was not used to being afraid of anyone. Hopefully invisible to the other, she shook off the feeling.

"What do you want from me, daughter of the sea goddess." The woman probably shook with laughter for a moment.

"Did you hear that little Raven, that's polite. Maybe you should take an example from her."

Her attention went from Ravana back to her. "I don't want anything from your child, because there's nothing you can give me. I just wanted to let you know that if you're looking for me I'm in Mountania." Not understanding, she tilted her head.

"Why are you telling me this?" Isodora spread her arms.

"Just if you want to talk now you know where to find me." After those words she disappeared into thin air. Turnog turned so quickly that Helana had to jump aside to let him pass.

"YOU TALKED TO HER." Ravana slapped the table with both hands, Turnog sat in a chair and listened to her. Helana was leaning against the wall opposite the table, she had gotten to know Ravana so well in such a short time that she kept out of this.

"She spoke to me and I asked what she was doing here. Nothing more was said." Ravana leaned further forward.

"Are you sure, there is nothing else you want to say?" He nodded a little uncertainly, but he nodded.

"You are hiding something." Both looked at Helana, she bit her lip for a moment to stay out of it, she walked to the table and sat down. "Isodora definitely told you something, maybe along the lines of the curse. I can only guess why you're keeping it hidden and my guess is that you don't know what it means." He nodded and closed his eyes.

"Did the gulls tell you that?" Ravana's look was full of amazement and if Helana had to be honest she was also amazed at herself, where did that wisdom suddenly come from. This was not for her, she shook her head, not for her at all. Ravana left her alone and turned her attention back to him.

"I hope you know what you're doing, my little brother. Because I can't always protect you, not like back then with Sval's death." He nodded again, but he kept his eyes closed. Apparently he did not want to talk about it any further and she could make good use of it, she frowned for a moment.

"But what those she want with me?" It was actually meant to put that question in her mind, but everyone was indeed looking at her. Turnog had also opened his eyes to look at her.

"I don't dare say that for sure, but may I ask you a question where is Mountania?" Helana lowered her eyes for a moment.

"It's a place beyond the bridge." Just like when she told who she was, everyone was shocked. "Since you disappeared, the gangs have also disappeared from that village and that allowed it to grow. So much so that they had to go through the mountains, my school is in Mountania." Obviously unhappy with that answer, Ravana hit the table again.

"Well that's one thing I do know, you have no business in that village across the bridge. You're not a member of the crew, but you live in my father's house and that's why I can say this to you."Not waiting for an answer, Ravana left the room.

"I'll put it differently Helana, whenever there were problems in this town the cause was always over the bridge. We lost our father to an attack by a gang who were after Ravana."

Helana swallowed, it was a lot like her situation.

"What do I have to look for there, everything that connects me to a village in that city has not yet been built." Turnog nodded for a moment, but he wasn't fully convinced yet.

"I hope you mean it, Helana." He sighed for a moment. "I really hope so."

One step closer

Turnog

Helana had fallen asleep at the table and Turnog couldn't bear to wake her up. Ravana hadn't come back since she stormed the house either, he wasn't worried about her. She could take excellent care of herself, better than anyone he knew or has known. Helana sighed in her sleep and he kept looking at her, even when she was a sleep she enchanted him and he had no other explanation for it. When Ravana had raged on him she had kept herself a little aloof, but when she noticed that he was hiding something from Ravana, she did not hold back. She could also have expressed in words what was going through him at that moment, normal was Ravana who knew him better than himself. But right at the moment, she radiated so much peace that it calmed him down too.

"Captain." Skegg entered the room, Turnog quickly put his index finger to his lips and pointed at her. Skegg nodded and beckoned him with his head. He took one last look at her, after his conversation with Skegg he would put her to bed.

"I'm really sorry Captain, I wanted to warn you about her. But this body is no longer what it once was, forgive me." Turnog put a hand on his shoulder.

"You have nothing to apologize for, I should have said this morning that I knew where the silver fox was." He used that nickname again, but this time he didn't have much trouble with it. Skegg nodded a moment, then shook his head.

"Then we can bear this shame together."

TURNOG WALKED WITH her in his arms, Skegg followed him.

"Apparently she was very tired, she doesn't even wake up from this." For a moment he was concerned that Skegg's loud voice would wake her up after all. But she kept her eyes closed even as he placed her gently on the bed and pulled the thin sheet over her.

"I'll just do the chores."Turnog frowned for a moment.

"Didn't I ask you to give those chores to someone else."Skegg nodded a moment.

"You did, but I didn't listen and the others have their own chores." He sighed and gently pushed Skegg out of the room.

"Come on, let's let her sleep." Before closing the door, he glanced at her, his heart leaping a little. Her eyes were wide open, her mouth shaped something.

"Thank you." Turnog nodded for a moment, then closed the door.

TURNOG RUBBED THE MOSAIC of reflective glass with a damp woolen cloth, his father had called it a mirror and he had simply taken the name.

"Well the wheel is oiled, should I just go and clean the windows?" Skegg already walked to the windows and ran a finger against the sanded glass.

"Yes they could use soapy water, I'll be right back." The sun was already setting, Ravana was still not back.

"Do that tomorrow, but Skegg it will be dark soon." Skegg also squinted now.

"You are probably right about that." But he walked away anyway, leaving him alone with his own thoughts. He looked at his broken reflection, he had never recognized his reflection. He saw his father in the mirror every time. Skegg's heavy steps betrayed him before he re-entered the lightroom, bucket in one hand and woolen cloth in the other.

"Have you seen my sister yet?" Skegg shook his head.

"But she will come back, she's probably on the road with Thunder. You know how she is and especially when Swawater comes up. She still blames herself for the death of your father." Turnog could only nod, he also blamed himself for being trapped in this dungeon.

"She and I are very similar in that." Skegg laughed for a moment, but shook his head.

"Why don't you teach the princess to ride a horse?" Turnog shrugged for a moment, it was a good idea. Yet another little shadow of doubt surfaced again, he didn't want to get too attached to her.

"Maybe it's not a good idea after all." Skegg shrugged.

"She's a guest not a prisoner, so it might be useful for her to be able to move around freely. Take Purco, that's a quiet little creature."

TURNOG LUGGED SOME logs for the stove, Skegg stirred a gigantic pan.

"I'll make soup, hopefully the princess likes it." Turnog shook his head wearily, he wasn't going to tell Skegg again not to get too close. But it was no use, and if he did it, he wasn't fair either, because he did exactly the same thing.

"Have you already decided on the lessons?"

"Lessons, what lessons." Ravana entered the kitchen. Her hair was filled with leaves and branches.

"I have suggested that the captain give the princess horse riding lessons." Ravana nodded slowly and went to the kitchen cupboards. She didn't like the idea at all, he could tell from her attitude. She left the kitchen with her hands full of service.

"I think she disagrees."Skegg's ever-observant comments never get boring.

"I'm going to wake up Helana, otherwise you will do all that effort for nothing." Turnog left the kitchen and looked around the house for a moment. The white walls and the dark wooden beams, the only decoration they had was the portrait. For the rest there was the dining table and a sofa on which people could sit. There wasn't even a rug on the floor, he could hardly imagine Summernight's widow having left everything like that. He wanted to muse on another time, but his stomach began to growl violently.

"HELANA." GENTLY TURNOG put his hand on her narrow shoulder and shook it slowly. She groaned in protest. "Helana, dinner is almost ready." She moaned, he slowly got a smile on his face. Once she was asleep, she was very difficult to wake up. "Come on, you can go back to sleep soon."

"Do you promise?" He fired softly, somewhere he had expected this reaction. Only not from her, it was normal something Ravana would ask him. He brushed the brown hair from her face, her blue eyes were still closed.

"I promise." Only then she opened her eyes and she could barely hide a yawn behind her hand. Turnog slowly stood up and reighed a hand to her, a little twinkle of doubt shone in her eyes, but she took it as she stood up. They were very close together, although his head was screaming for him to take a step back, he stopped. She didn't move either, she closed her eyes for a moment and swallowed.

"Captain, princess. The food is on the table." Skegg's voice found its way upstairs. Turnog sighed for a moment, then reluctantly moved. He went down the stairs to her and offered her his arm at the bottom of the stairs. But she shook her head gently and he shrugged slowly.

"RAVANA, ARE YOU ALL right?" Turnog was really worried, she hadn't said anything for the entire meal. She didn't even look up when he asked, clearly her thoughts were elsewhere.

"Aren't you hungry?" It was Helana who asked her the question, he had indeed noticed that she had not even touched the soup. But they responded at all, Helana reighed her hand into that of Ravana and patted it gently. Only then Ravana seemed to wake up, looking uncertainly at him and Helana. Helana then asked again if she was not hungry, Ravana sighed.

"I'm sorry, I'm not a nice company." She quickly took a bite of the now cold vegetable soup.

"It doesn't matter, Ravana, we all have days like that." Helana nodded in agreement.

"Will Skegg mind if I don't help with the dishes today?"

"He doesn't mind." Skegg waddled into the room, Ravana gave him a grateful smile. Helana got up and helped Skegg clean up.

"I'll help him, I'll be a guest here. I can still help." Turnog turned his attention back to his sister.

"Are you going to the watchtower again tonight?" Ravana just nodded and then got up.

"Don't worry about me, it's my job to take care of you." He shook his head.

"Mother would have wanted us to watch each other." He felt her anger grow, he should not have said this. Even though he stood by his words, all he could do now was watch her run out of the house.

SKEGG POKED HIS HEAD through the door for a moment.

"I'm going back to the lighthouse captain." Before he could argue or wish him a good evening, he was gone. Not much later, Helana came out of the kitchen, her eyes twinkled. Skegg had probably made some of his famous jokes again.

"So you've eaten and now you can go back to sleep." She froze for a moment, then nodded.

"I forgot that for a while." Turnog got up slowly and then walked over to her.

"If you can still take it, can I have this dance?" He surprised himself with this question, because he couldn't dance at all.

"But there is no music." He raised his index finger and immediately the sounds of a violin drifted down.

"You didn't think Skegg could only cook and make good jokes. No, he also plays the violin."

She started to laugh.

"Is there anything that man can't do?" Turnog looked dubious.

"Certainly yes, but I haven't found it yet." And he also started to laugh. He reached out to her for the second time in the evening and for the second time in the evening she took it. He pulled her towards him and they shuffled across the room together.

"I should probably warn you, because I can't dance at all." She looked at him in surprise.

"Then why did you ask me to dance?" He raised his shoulders.

"I wanted to dance, tomorrow you will get riding lessons from me." That surprised look in her eyes again, it was the most beautiful thing he had ever seen and that meant something.

"Thank you." Her voice trembled a little, tears were in her eyes.

"What's the matter, don't you think it's a good idea?" She nodded.

"I am very grateful to you, it is just that my father and I did this often. Dancing, I mean, my mother played the piano and we would dance across the room." His good humor faded a little.

"I am again sorry about your parents. I would like to explain to you what happens to us when we go to the other realm, we are then overcome by an irrevocable urge for violence and blood. We cannot contain ourselves and we cannot. staying here." Helana closed her eyes for a moment, he immediately felt guilty. She put her head against his chest and sighed.

"I wish I could help you break the curse." Turnog bit his lip and closed his eyes.

"Really don't know what you could do." He put his head gently on his hair, this felt good. Better than he hoped.

"SKEGG HAS STOPPED PLAYING." Turnog raised his head and saw that she was right, slowly she took a step back.

"I think I'll just go to bed." Turnog would like her to stay with him a little longer. Helana walked away from him, but turned to face him at the stairs. She ran over to him, jumped up and kissed him on the cheek. "Thanks for the dance. You didn't get on my feet once." Turnog gave her a smile, she wanted to walk away again. But he took her arm and pulled her towards him. She put her hand on his chest. "What are you doing?" Turnog leaned forward and pressed his lips to his hair. His body again flooded with this good feeling, she did not withdraw. Helana was just pushing her lips against his.

Riding lessons

Helana

Helana was sitting straight on the back of the light gray mare, she had already had lessons for a few weeks. But she still couldn't keep an attitude. He rode next to her and laughed at her sore face.

"You are a natural." She looked his way a little angrily, which made him laugh more.

"Stop laughing, it's not funny." As she says it, the mare makes a little jump, causing her to let out another little cry. He just barely rolled off his own horse with laughter. Pleasant tears streamed down his cheeks and cleared a path on the dust-stained face.

HER WHOLE BODY BEGGED to dismount, not only Turnog lay double in thought, Helana also heard her grandfather.

"A Summernight never gives up when it started something." With a thin smile she urged the animal to speed up a bit, Turnog had advanced for a moment and at a light trot she stumbled behind it.

"Can't we just walk?"She bit her lip and squeezed the reins a little hard, which was not appreciated. He examined her closely, then shook his head.

"Just keep biting and then you don't feel it anymore." She frowned, what would she not feel? Her stiff muscles, or the blisters that had appeared on her stern. Maybe both, as she might fall off her horse from fatigue. Helana had not yet managed to sleep well all night, something she was not used to. She let go of the bridle with one hand to suppress a yawn.

"I heard that!" Helana rolled her eyes for a moment and sighed. He had asked several times if she was okay and each time she had brushed it off. Still, she was not comfortable with the fatigue, as was the tangible distance between him and her. Turno hadn't touched her since the kiss, he didn't seem to dare anymore. Ravana was also a bit more distant, Skegg on the other hand was still very friendly, but something had changed in him too. It was not in his manner, but in the way he looked at her.

"Do you feel yourself being pushed up?" She nodded and knew what that meant, slowly rose and then sat down again.

"You see, I think that should help." She nodded reluctantly, helping her sore muscles by souring further.

AT LAST THEY WERE BACK at the lighthouse, Skegg was already coming out.

"Captain and princess, how was the ride?" Skegg took hold of the reins of her horse so Helana could dismount. As soon as Helana hit the ground, she felt a little light in her head, she shook her head for a moment and took a deep breath.

"I have nothing to complain about, but Helana." Both men turned their attention to her, something she couldn't use now. "Helana?" Turnog was already walking over to her, she quickly raised her head and shook her head.

"No, but like you said, I'm starting to learn." His eyes narrowed, he probably saw her. But she was not allowed to show him that she felt weak, she was ashamed of it. She quickly took the reins of the mare and wanted to accompany the animal to the stable.

"Leave it to me, princess." said Skeg, the reins were removed from her hands. "You go in and drink some of your special tea. I've already put on some water."Helana wanted to argue, but something in his look stopped her.

"Thanks, I'll put it right away for you too." Both men shook their heads.

"We still have to muck out the stables and there are other things that require our attention."

Helana sighed, this was also something they were doing lately.

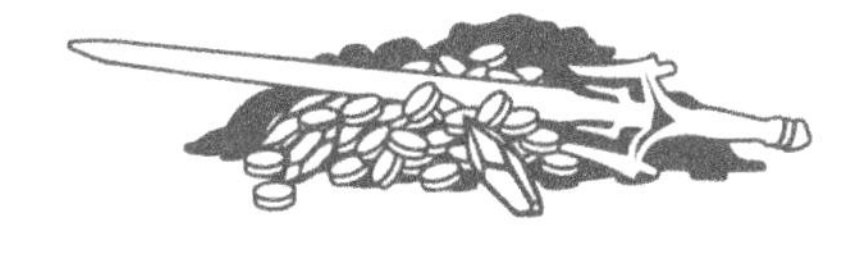

WITH A LITTLE RELUCTANCE Helana walked into the house, there was indeed a kettle on the stove in the kitchen. She took a mug from the cupboard and put the tea in a bag.

"Ah, poor child." Startled, she turned, there was no one else in the kitchen. She recognized the voice, it was Isodora's. "They avoid you as if you had a contagious disease." Her gaze went across the kitchen again.

"Show yourself, witch. I'm not in the mood for games." A giggle came through the kitchen.

"Good to know, but if you don't mind, I'd rather not run the chance that Turnog sees me. He and I are not good friends." Helana rolled her eyes for a moment, this was no secret. She also knew why.

"If only you shouldn't have had it both ways with my ancestor." The laughter died down.

"I had forgotten for a moment that you descended from Captain Summernight and that you were brought up on this story. Only you are wrong with one thing, I did not cheat on Turnog with the captain. But with his son." Helana shook her head.

"That really makes the difference, really now I understand you completely." Something gripped her arm, it squeezed very hard, but she didn't want to budge.

"Have I asked for your pity, do you think you are waiting for your tasteless jokes."Her hand went to where she felt a grip. Her hand took hold of her arm and with great difficulty she pulled it off her own arm.

"If you can't take that, maybe you should go. As was made clear earlier, you are not welcome here and I understand why." Helana let go of the arm and looked into the void where she suspected the witch was standing.

"You are only going to feel worse and they know it. This realm is taking away your life energy, no matter how strong your soul may be. That tea is a good move but it is only temporary. The other women did not survive the third full moon. " She gasped, was that actually why the others were distant.

"You are lying."

"WHO ARE YOU TALKING to?" Ravana entered the kitchen, it felt as if she had been caught. Ravana looked around the kitchen in amazement.

"Isodora, she was here." Ravana's eyes widened and she looked around the kitchen again for the witch.

"Where is she now?" Helana shrugged and sighed.

"I couldn't see her, but believe me when I say she was here." Ravana nodded.

"I believe you, she's a master of tricks. That's why she's nicknamed the silver fox." Ravana had mentioned the nickname before and had tried the name a few times herself, but it always left a strange taste in her mouth.

"What did she want?" The question was normal, except it sounded very hostile.

"She wanted to talk." Ravana clenched her fists, a fire burned behind her eyes.

"What did she want to talk about?" Again that hostile tone, it was not comfortable for her.

"She wanted to talk about me, she told me I'm only going to feel worse and you already knew." The anger in her own voice astonished her, but the reaction on Ravana's face only ignited the anger in her.

"SO SHE WAS TELLING the truth?" Helana looked at the faces of the other at the dinner table, Ravana had fetched them after she exploded.

"I'll kill that witch again." This was the first time she'd heard Skegg talk like that, yet she felt the same rage burning inside her.

"I want to go back to my own realm." Turnog slid forward slightly and rested his elbows on the table.

"And with love I had brought you there, but unfortunately you would not survive the journey." She looked at him in disbelief.

"Then you kill me just like you killed my parents." He shook his head, Ravana stood open and put a hand on Skegg's shoulder.

"Come on, let's finish the stables. These two can handle this conversation on their own."

Turnog shook his head for a moment.

"Go Skegg, Ravana is right. He and I can handle this." Skegg was visibly unhappy about it, but she meant what she said. She wanted to hear it from Turnog's mouth and Ravana and Skegg had better not be there. Skegg got up and walked out of the house with Ravana.

HELANA'S EYES NARROWED, she turned her attention back to him and he sighed.

"We cannot take you into your own realm because you will not survive it. Not because we will kill you, but because this realm will not let you go until it has your full life force." Helana tilted her head slightly, this was not really an explanation but, meanwhile, she was trying to decipher the look on his face.

"In other words, I was already doomed when you took me on board?" Turnog nodded slowly. She dropped her head into her hands, how could she have been so stupid. They had only brought her here to die, only the unexplained gracious death of her parents but a slow death. "Why?" Turnog raised his shoulders.

"We don't know, it's just like we have that unknown hunger for blood. We have to take every young woman we find with us. We've tried to stop ourselves, but nothing seems to help." Helana raised her head and hit the table with both hands flat.

"I understand there is nothing you can do about it, it's the curse, but what I want to know is why you didn't tell me before. Everyone here says I have a strong soul, but why did you keep this from me." He didn't respond, she felt her cheeks burn with rage. He didn't even look at her, he felt ashamed, because he had judged her less or only now saw that she was stronger than she looked. She wanted to know and she got up. Her hands buried her hair and she sighed. "Turnog, talk to me. I am not magical powers and therefore cannot read minds."

"To my knowledge, witches cannot do that either." She screamed and turned away from him, he intended to change the subject.

"You are the dragon of the sea, but you don't even answer my question!" Only now did he look at her and she did not know if she was mistaken, but according to her she saw tears shining in his eyes in the fading daylight.

"I really wanted to tell you, but every time it just speeded up the process." She swallowed her anger for a moment, she wanted to understand that he was doing it for her, but she still wasn't satisfied with that. He sighed and hung his head. "I know, but I didn't mean to scare you." Helana shook her head and sat back on the chair with a sigh.

"As you can see, I don't feel good enough to be afraid, or maybe I'm just too angry to be afraid." He started to laugh, it was a nervous laugh, but it was enough to break the tense atmosphere in the room. She couldn't help but laugh with him, gasped for a moment. Helana was very angry with him just a moment ago and now she was smiling. "But that still doesn't explain why, Isodora told me about it. What can she gain from it." Turnog also stopped laughing now and lowered everything.

"I think because she hates me and wants to turn you against me."

"AGAINST US, TURNOG. She's trying to turn you against us. That's something she likes turning people against each other. She tried to do that with us and with you and Sval." Ravana came back into the house, Helana frowned slightly. Sval she had heard that name before, she just couldn't remember where. She wanted to ask Turnog, but his gaze was so dark that she left it behind.

"She even took pleasure in pitting Captain Summernight against you, for no good reason."

"What my grandfather used to tell you is that you held her prisoner against her will." Turnog's eyes widened.

"What stories did your grandfather tell you?" She shrugged lightly, it pleased her to think about her grandfather.

"Especially sea stories, but this was family history and unlike my father I was a good listener." Turnog sighed and then laughed again, joined him again. Ravana looked at them in surprise, but then also joined.

"What's there to laugh about?"

Ravana's View

Ravana, during the conversation

Ravana was not surprised that the silver fox tried to turn Helana against Turnog. But telling her she didn't have much longer to live was low even for that witch. But what really surprised her was that the witch had the guts to do that in her father's house. She was standing in the stable with Thunder, brushing his already shiny coat with a soft brush. It helped her think and she could immediately put her frustration into it.

"Are you alright?" Skegg entered the stable, she shook her head.

"No, I understand why Helana is so angry with us. We shouldn't have kept this from her." He just nodded and sighed. He did not pick up a brush, but a fork.

"Are you going to muck out the stables now?" He nodded again.

"That calms me down and we can't let those animals sleep in a dirty bed." Ravana laughed, but it sounded hallow in her own ears.

"Then just remove the dirty spots, tomorrow I'll help you with the whole picture." Skegg nodded reluctantly.

"I'll hold you to that."

"WHAT WILL THEY TALK about?" Ravana looked at the stable door.

"You can guess that, Helana wants to answer and she will do everything to get it." Like Skegg, she wanted to know what was happening there, for a while she felt like she should tell Helana why she was feeling so tired and weak. But the girl kept herself tall all the time, especially when she was on a horse. Skegg's soft cough brought her back to the stable.

"She looked so good today until she got off the horse and turned very pale." Ravana saw him shake his head.

"It's not fair why this realm is attacking her, but not us." She wish she could answer that question, but she didn't know. Even her ability to see magic failed her in this.

"I wish I knew Skegg, I wish I knew. But my eye." Ravana was referring to her green eye, which she normally hid behind a tuft of hair.

"I know girl, she hasn't been doing his job since we've been in this dungeon. Maybe it's because we're no longer alive." Ravana dropped the brush from her hands, never thought about it that way.

"Do you really think so?" He rested on the wooden part of the fork.

"Of course I mean that, it explains a lot." She bent down to pick up the brush and had to admit he had a good point. If she was no longer alive, it explained why the world attacked their life force.

"It explains a lot, but not everything." He gave her a puzzled look and pointed to the horses.

"Then what are they doing here? They weren't on the ship when we were hit by lightning."

Skegg sighed and frowned, the wrinkles forming on his forehead. She patted Thunder's neck and sighed there was nothing more she could do here, Skegg was almost done cleaning out the three stables.

"I'M GOING IN, HOPEFULLY those two have finished talking." Skegg nodded and tossed the last heap of horse manure into a wagon with a wheel. Which he invented, he called it a wheelbarrow, and he brought the manure to the wind farms.

"That is nutrition for the plants." Ravana should not remember that the food she puts in her mouth grows on animal or human shit. She shook these thoughts out of her head and started to walk into the house, listening at the door just in case. She heard her brother laugh and that warmed her heart, because he hadn't done that in ages.A feminine laughter mingled with his, tears sprang lightly to her eyes. Helana was a much better woman to Turnog than Isodora ever was. The laughter died down and Helana asked him what the silver fox was trying to achieve. She stormed in without thinking.

Sleep

Turnog

Turnog sat on a stool in the corner of the room, listening to her calm breathing. He shook his face with an incredulous smile. What did that woman do to him, she changed him and he couldn't do anything about it. Helana had said something about him and he knew from an unreliable source that it is not something magical. Something he didn't believe, all he had to do was look at her and his heart skipped a beat. All he had to do was listen to her and he could no longer consent. A small knock on the door woke him from his thoughts, the door opened softly and Ravana's head came through. Her gaze went straight to him and not to the young woman sleeping in the bed, but she looked straight at him.

"Is she sleeping?" He nodded and looked at her.

"The question is only for how long?" Ravana nodded a moment and looked at Helana.

"I know what you mean." Ravana had probably heard Helana wandering around at night.

"I can watch over her, you need your sleep." He shook his head, he didn't want to part from Helana.

"No, I'll stay here. Go to bed." Ravana wanted to argue with him, he could tell from her expression, but probably changed her mind. She disappeared from the doorway and the door was pulled shut.

TURNOG WAS ALONE AGAIN with his thoughts and those that took him to that afternoon. He admired her fiery rage when she confronted him with withholding information and he couldn't blame her, she wouldn't back down by leaps and bounds like the other women had done. Still, she had turned a bit paler and sometimes a bit quieter version of herself, and the second full moon was approaching. She was already beginning to curl and flounder, as soon as he could he got up and walked over to her. She jerked up. Her eyes stared into nowhere for a moment, while her mouth plugs open but no sound came out. He sat on the bed and put his arms around her, as Ravana had always done with him when he was little and had a nightmare. Her heart pounded against his chest, he moved slowly back and forth. She clung to him and began to sob.

"Calm down, I will not let anything happen to you." Helana pushed away from him and looked at him with her big blue eyes.

"That is a lie, you can't protect me against this realm." Turnog nodded, she was right about that.

"I promise I would do everything I could to keep you alive." She continued to look at him in disbelief but then fell back into his arms, sobbing again.

"I want to believe you, really." He stroked her hair.

"I'll stay here until you fall asleep again." Helana nodded and settled back into her pillow. Her eyes closed and her breath calmed down.

"Thank you." He stroked her hair and gave her a smile she couldn't see.

"TURNOG." A SLENDER hand landed on his shoulder, his eyes darted. Sunlight filled the room, Turnog blinked a moment. Helana was standing in front of him, already dressed and hair combed. He came forward cautiously, every muscle in his body screaming with stiffness.

"Good morning." Her amused smile made him forget the pain in his muscles, he only had eyes for her. Helana looked visibly better than yesterday, a little less pale, and the dark blue bags under her eyes were disappearing.

"Good morning to you too, how are you feeling?" Helana shrugged and sighed.

"May I say I don't know, I slept better but otherwise." He motioned for her to move back slightly so that he could get up from the wooden stool.

"At least you slept better, that's a good start." He stretched and found his stomach growling. Helana probably heard it because she laughed. She was so close to him and he could no longer resist taking her in his arms. She didn't resist, she put two hands on his chest. Her blue eyes were on his lips, he slowly moved his face to hers.

A COUGH MADE HIM LOOK up, not knowing how long they had stood there. Ravana stood in the doorway with folded arms.

"Breakfast is ready." Helana pushed free and walked away from him, Turnog wanted to follow her but was stopped by Ravana.

"Have you gone mad?" Turnog didn't quite understand her, she meant the kiss. She kept staring at him and sighed.

"You have made a promise that you probably cannot keep." He shook his head, she probably heard him. She was right as almost always, but he did start to irritate her.

"That's not to say I'm not going to try and I think Helana knows that too." It was her turn to sigh, lowering her eyes in frustration.

"Come on, eat something and then you have to send the men on the Steria. Tomorrow there is a full moon and you know what that means." He nodded and started to walk past her, she grabbed his arm.

"Please look out of Turnog." He ripped his arm free.

"I know what I am doing." He went down the stairs.

"I hope so."

Truth or delusion

Helana

Turnog didn't say much when he sat across from her at the table, in fact, he had regained the habit of not saying anything to her while he was eating.

"Come on, Captain, we have to go." Skegg walked from the kitchen to the front door, not even looking up or around.

"Good morning Skegg too." He froze for a moment, then walked on, looking at Turnog, who shrugged for a moment.

"I thought we had broken the silence." Turnog took a bite of his sandwich and then got up too, walking with long strides to the door.

"Turnog?" He stopped his hand on the doorknob.

"Will I see you tonight?" Turnog jerked open the door, but he did not walk through.

"The moon is full tomorrow and we have to set sail, I think you should know."

Helana wanted to go in but already walked through the door and slammed the door behind him.

"HE IS AFRAID." RAVANA came down the stairs, Helana gave her a puzzled look.

"How do you mean?" Ravana walked over to her and leaned both hands on the table, a slight mockery on her face.

"For a smart person, that's a stupid question." All she could do was nod in agreement. It was a stupid question, he was clearly afraid she would be gone when he got back.

"I'm not going anywhere, at least not voluntarily." All Ravana could nod was, she straightened up and sighed.

"I will also go to the ship in the same way, can you manage here on your own?" Helana just nodded, she could always come up with something to do.

"Worry about me, but don't worry I won't walk in seven seas at once." A thin smile appeared on Ravana's face.

"I hope you are right, as my brother said we are going back to your empire tomorrow night. Unfortunately we cannot take you with us and you are left here alone. We also cannot leave anyone behind." Helana raised her hand and now stood up too.

"Again, this realm doesn't get me down that easily, at least when I run out of tea, I'm going to worry anyway." Ravana laughed and she joined her too. Ravana quit much too soon.

"I know what my brother has promised you. You should know that he will do anything to make it happen." Helana just nodded and sighed, taking a sip of her tea.

"I know that and I also know that it will not be easy. Is there really no one who has more information?" Ravana shrugged.

"Not to my knowledge, I suspect only Isodora knows and I don't trust a word that leaves her mouth." Helana tightened her grip on her cup, she knew Ravana was right. Isodora was the only one who might have all the answers.

RAVANA HAD LEFT HER alone and deep in thought Helana had done the dishes. But now she was standing on the cliff again, listening to the screams of fighting seagulls in the air. It offered rest, but rest was not much to her. Answers were more useful for her, maybe she could help him keep his promise. Knowing he wouldn't forgive himself if something happened to her, she squeezed her hands into fists and turned away from the sea. She no longer heard the gulls, she walked in a straight line to the stables. The horses stood with their heads outside the boxes, the light gray mare nodded a few times when she saw Helana.

"We're going for a ride." Helana opened the horse box and let the mare walk out. As fast as she could, she rigged the animal and mounted it. She bit her lip for a moment, unsure if she was doing the right thing. But what other choice did she have, it was her life that slowly faded away. She urged the animal and immediately regretted her decision, the animal rushed ahead. Much faster than she had ever been, what Turnog called this speed again. She shook her head and sat firmly in the saddle, afraid that at this speed she would lose her balance and fall off. But unlike the trot, which hurt a lot, this went very easily and almost painlessly. Soon she drove past the mills of the sky farms, a charred wooden tower she did not know stood at the edge of the forest. She wanted to know what had happened here, but stopping to investigate was something she couldn't afford.

The clatter of hooves on the narrow bridge was now behind her. The mountains that once dominated the landscape now surrounded her. The silted path led to a village, with dilapidated wooden houses. She pulled slightly on the reins to slow the animal, looking in amazement at the village that was a crude shadow of the town in which she had grown up. The houses were deserted, the doors hung crooked in their posts. Not knowing what to think of this they drove through the village, she got a strange-looking tower in the eye. It was not built of wood, but of white rock. It looked very suspicious and new, so she drove to it. She was almost at the front door when it flew open, Isodora was in the doorway.

"Helana Summernight, what a nice surprise. I was already starting to think you wouldn't come again." Helana climbed out of the saddle with great difficulty, holding onto the mare's reins.

"Let's just say I'm not here to socialize, I have questions and to my knowledge you're the only one with answers." All Isodora could do was nod.

"Put your horse in the stable, I'll see what I can do for you."

THEY WERE IN THE LIVING room of the tower, which was decorated with different fabrics, all in a sea blue color. Isodora poured tea into porcelain cups.

"Well let me guess, you want to know more about how to stay alive." Helana shrugged slightly, of course it was the only reason she was here. Isodora brought her cup to her mouth and sipped the still hot liquid.

"Let me get you out of the dream of a cure right away, because there is none." Helana had to admit that she was slightly disappointed, but immediately what Ravana had said this morning came to her mind.

"How do I know you're not lying, you don't have to help me." Isodora dropped her cup with a loud bang, the hot liquid sloshing over the edges. Helana raised an eyebrow and stared at the witch.

"I'm not wrong, you are not really the most trustworthy person." Isodora studied her, then nodded.

"You are indeed right, but don't forget girl. You came to me and not the other way around."

"Actually that's not true, you invited me." Helana sat a little more comfortably on the ottoman, missing the wooden chairs in the lighthouse house now, Isodora chuckled and nodded.

"You do have a strong soul and you have a good brain. Something your ancestors missed. But enough about them, I can tell you I only speak the truth. I swear on my mother Tishilla goddess of the sea." Still with a slight suspicion, Helana nodded.

"Isn't there any way to stop this?" A sparkle shot through the witch's eyes.

"There is only one way and that is to break this curse." Helana 's eyes widened, her mouth slowly opened.

"Breaking the curse, how?" Isodora leaned forward slightly, the pillow creaking under the movement. With a simple movement she pushed the cup of cold tea towards her.

"Don't let it get cold." Helana quickly picked up the cup and began to drink the tea. As soon as she put the cup down, Isodora wanted to refill it. She quickly put her hand over her cup.

"You were talking about breaking the curse." Isodora's eyes narrowed a little, it seemed as if she was irritated, because Helana was not giving her what she wanted.

“Breaking the curse is not easy. I accidentally made this curse because Turnog killed the man I loved. So to break this curse it takes a blood sacrifice and I don't mean a few drops that would are too easy.” Helana swallowed, she really didn't want to hear the rest, but Isodora paid no attention to that and went on.

"One of you must give your life." Helana's shoulders slumped, she wouldn't believe what she'd just heard. The only thing that could save her was if Turnog gave his life for hers. She shook her head, no she wouldn't believe it. The stories did not go that way, the two lovers survived everything because their love was so powerful. Tears sprang to her eyes and bit her lip.

"Like I said I would only speak the truth and I did." Helana stood and walked back and forth for a moment.

"I don't believe you, I can't believe you." All the witch did was drink from her cup again.

"I can't force you to believe me, but somehow you know what I've told you is true." Helana shook her head again.

"I shouldn't have come." Helana was already walking to the door.

"What are you going to tell him?" Helena stopped with her hand pressed against the door.

"To be honest, that's none of your business." She pushed open the door and walked through.

HELANA JUMPED IN AN almost fluid movement, on the back of the light gray mare, she did not look back at the door of the tower. As she galloped away, Isodora did have a point. She had promised never to cross the stone bridge, so she knew the others would be angry she went. Again the hooves echoed on the stone bridge. Her eyes were fixed on the charred watchtower. She sighed with relief when she saw the white buildings of Truport, she was almost back where she should be. Yet for some reason she held back her horse, she had only given the animal a rest while she was drinking tea with Isodora. It did not seem fair to let the animal run any further, while also getting there at a slower pace.

"Here you are." Helana turned her head to see Skegg standing with his arms folded between the trees.

"When we get back you have a few things to explain." She nodded and now let the mare come to a complete stop.

"I didn't expect anything else." Skegg walked over to her, his slow pace took a while. He reached for the reins and patted the mare's neck with a soft hand.

"Don't you want to know where I was and why?"

He shook his head slowly from side to side.

"I know where you were and why you were there, to be honest if I were in your shoes I would have done it too. That's not to say tha captain is going to make it easier for you when he finds out, not to mention Ravana." She could only sigh

"Is there any possibility that I can speak to him alone?" He shook his head again.

"I'm sorry princess, but no." They arrived at the lighthouse, the door flew open. Turnog and Ravana crowded into the opening to run out first. The sun was already low in the sky, which meant she had been away longer than she expected.

"Where was she?" Skegg raised his hand.

"Let her get off first and then I can take care of this good girl." Again he patted the animal's neck, which shook its head wildly.

"It looks like she thinks it's a good idea." With a slight effort, thanks to tired muscles, she dismounted and walked over to the two concerned people.

"Let me get straight to the point, everything is going well for me. Except that the realm is still tapping into my life energy." Turnog breathed a sigh of relief, but Ravana needed more conviction.

"That doesn't explain why you were gone." Helana nodded and pointed inside.

"I think for what I have to tell you, we better sit down." Turnog and Ravana looked at each other.

"SO TELL." HELANA WAS sitting across from Turnog, Ravana had stepped up behind her. Turnog reached out to her.

"Please tell us where you were." She pulled her hands back and sighed, she couldn't go back now.

"I know how badly you want to fulfill your promise to protect me. But for that you need answers and no one here had them." She glanced over her shoulder at Ravana, whose posture tightened.

"That's why I went to the only one who has these answers." Turnog was starting to get it too.

"You don't mean that, you went to her!" She nodded slowly and sighed.

"I can say I'm sorry, but I'd be lying." She searched her mind for the following words, for she didn't have to look at Ravana to know that she was boiling with rage. "She had some answers, but I'm not sure yet if she was telling the truth."

"Of course she wasn't telling the truth, anything that comes out of the silver fox's mouth is a lie until proven otherwise." Ravana's voice was loud and filled with restrained rage, Turnog raised his hand.

"Calm Ravana, let her tell what the silver fox said. Then we can judge if they are lies." Ravana clapped her hands on the table, leaned forward and stared at Turnog intently.

"Do you know a way to keep her alive?" Ravana sighed and shook her head.

"No, everything I knew has done nothing in the past." Ravana pulled back a chair and sat down with a thud. "What did she say?" Ravana said it so reluctantly that Helana almost wanted to say that it was all nonsense after all.

"There is no way to keep me alive longer than the third full moon, that is our deadline and not a day. I can only be saved if the curse is broken, according to Isodora at least." Ravana grinned briefly, turning her attention to Ravana.

"Isodora also told you how to do that?" Helana nodded slowly.

"This is where I question her words, but she says the only way to break the curse is through a blood sacrifice." She looked at Turnog and he swallowed. "Because you killed her lover, must you or the one you love die to break the curse."

Ravana's choice

Ravana

Ravana sighed, her brother had a familiar look in his eyes. Something she hated, because that meant he believed the word of Isodora.

"You don't believe this. Every time you have a glimmer of happiness." Ravana shook her head and hit the table with her flat hand. A glimmer of regret sparkled in his gaze, yet the look of faith remained.

"But do you have a better idea." She squeezed her hand into a fist, this was something she hadn't thought about yet. She had the greatest knowledge of magic among anyone here, she cursed that she saw no other solution than the one the silver fox had given them.

"But why, why is Isodora only now giving us this answer." She knew the others didn't have this answer either. This was once again the case that only Isodora knew the answer.

"Well then we can only do one thing." Her brother looked at her in surprise.

"And that is?" Ravana looked at Helana, who gave her an uncertain look, which slightly restored her confidence in Helana.

"We have to make sure you both live."

"You mean until the third full moon?" Ravana got up without saying anything, something came to her mind and she did not want to know if her suspicion was correct. Still, she wanted to be on the safe side.

THEY RAN UP THE STAIRS and went to her room. For a moment she looked around, where had she left it. The walls were covered with various weapons, which she scrubbed daily with a woolen cloth. It was something Dad would be proud of, she could say for sure. She went to her desk where the cloth was, she pulled one of the drawers. With a lot of effort it slid open, there she only found more woolen cloths. With a little less effort, she closed it again and opened the drawer on the other side of the desk, which slid a little easier than the previous one. A white box became visible, she had not seen it in years. With a little hesitation she took it out, opening the box just to be sure. When she set head necklace with the sea green diamond, it was the last payment Mother had received. The man was a nice man, but had to wait his turn. She had already offered him a few drinks until he talked about the legend of the sea green diamond. It was a gift from the sea goddess to her first daughter, but when she died, the diamond passed from hand to hand. He also said that the diamond provided protection from the sea itself. When he showed the diamond to her, to boast, her eye had immediately seen the magic. She had begged mother not to give the diamond to her pimp, luckily the man who gave her the diamond was very drunk and had told the pimp that he had paid with normal gold pieces. Something that worked out very well.

WHEN FATHER TOOK THEM here, she found the head necklace with an empty holder that could hold a gem. He hadn't noticed and wasn't even angry when she told him about her deed almost a year later. She sat in the chair by the desk, he was just glad she had found something. He had never admitted it openly, but although mother was a woman of pleasure, he probably loved her. She just didn't know if it was because she was the only woman who had bore him a son or if it was because of her mother's beauty. She looked up and saw herself in the mirror, according to father she looked a lot like her mother. Except her eyes, because the one sea-green eye that saw magic was always an eyesore in her father's side. According to Isodora, she rolled her eyes. It was because it was the sign of watered down sea witch's blood, something her father didn't want to know about. She actually sighed she didn't want to part with the jewelry, but if this kept Helana safe for the time being then she had to. She sighed again and got up from the bed.

RAVANA WALKED OUT OF the room, she was at the top of the spiral staircase. Doubt struck again, she wanted to turn around and put the head chain back where she had got it from

"Turnog?" Helana's voice made her freeze in her action, the uncertainty in her voice she had never heard before.

"What is it, Helana?" Her brother's voice was cool, something she could understand.Helana had gone where she was not allowed to go and it made her own blood boil when she thought about it. But she could also understand why she had done it, she could not give her the answer she needed.

"Never mind it is nothing." Ravana swallowed for a moment.

"I'm sorry I didn't mean to be blunt, but you've betrayed my trust" The scraping of wooden chair legs on the stone floor became clearly audible.

"I have betrayed your trust? Tell me why should I trust you, you are the one who brought me here. While you knew I was going to die and you expect me to lean back." Ravana nodded approvingly, those were strong words and had they not spoken to her brother she probably would have let it go. She set her foot on the bottom steps, which, as usual, creaked terribly. Without thinking further she continued down the stairs, two pairs of eyes looked at her.

"Helana, you have a good point." Ravana folded her arms. "But we told you not to come there and you went anyway. But you came back with answers, which I did not expect. Even though we are not sure if these answers are true." She walked to the table.

"The only thing I can think of is why the silver fox told you this is to see if we hurt you. If we don't then I have no doubt she will take matters into her own hands. the only way to get to Turnog is to let him live with a broken heart." Turnog leaned back slightly.

"What do you mean?" Ravana sighed.

"Just as I say it, Isodora would do anything to hurt you and that's something I can't let happen." He just nodded and then looked at Helana.

"Then we better do everything we can to keep you safe." Helana shook her head.

"Maybe it would be better if you kill me now, the curse is broken."

Soul of the sea

Turnog

Turnog shook his head in disbelief, he heard it right. If she was willing to die for him, he shook his head again. He could not allow this, everything in him called to oppose it.

"We have to look at all the options before we make that decision. All we you know that what you told the silver fox a lie." He frowned for a moment, shaking off the feeling of helplessness. Still, he couldn't shake a glimmer of the feeling. "Plus, we can't expect you to sacrifice yourself for us. After everything we've done to you." Turnog remembered what she had just said and she was right. She wasn't the one to gain the trust, that was his job.

"You were right." Helana tilted her head slightly.

"What was I right about." He rolled his eyes, why did she want to hear exactly where she was right. She couldn't just take the compliment and let it rest.

"You were right about trust." She nodded briefly with a simple movement.

TURNOG SAW THE JEWELRY and swallowed what he wanted to say. But he tried to look his sister in the eye, but every time he almost succeeded she looked away from him again. She had just been up there for a long time, probably fought her doubts and she still hadn't won. Helana sighed and sat back in the chair from which she had just gotten up.

"But if you set sail tomorrow, how can you protect me?" Ravana froze for a second, but quickly recovered.

"For starters, you wear this." Ravana held out the jewelry, Helana looked at it in amazement. Ravana sighed when Helana didn't take it, she walked over to the young woman and placed the head chain on her head.

"The diamond in this piece of jewelry is known as the soul of the sea." Loud gasp filled the room, he should have known she had heard several stories about it.

"If that's true why are you giving it to me?" Helana had turned to Ravana, who shrugged. He could see she saw tears in her eyes, it hurt her more than she might want to admit. Helana had seen this too, and her hands went straight to the jewelry.

"I can't accept it, not even to borrow." Turnog had a thin smile on his face, he was proud of Helana. Ravana had the same reaction, probably because Helana said she actually borrowed the jewelry.

"You keep the jewelry on your head, then tomorrow I will board a little more confidently."

Helana wanted to go there again, but he got some up from his chair and reached out to her. He took her hand, she looked at him uncertainly and he shook his head.

HELANA HAD LEFT FOR her bedroom completely exhausted, leaving him and Ravana alone.

"You get it back." Ravana sat in Helana's chair and nodded slowly.

"Would it help?" Turnog shrugged, he didn't want to lie to her saying he didn't trust it, but he didn't know for sure.

"Time will tell, but I also feel better now that I know she is wearing the diamond." Ravana nodded slowly and sighed.

"Mother would have understood, right?" He took her hands, just as he had taken Helana's before.

"If she were still with us she would have understood and she would even have been proud of you." Ravana shook her head in disbelief.

"I can't believe it did. I've given away the soul of the sea." He squeezed her arm gently.

"You lent it, it will come back to you when all this is over." She bit her lip and was clearly not convinced yet.

"Ravana, it will not be easy. But it is actually time to go to sleep, tomorrow we sail out and I have you rested and I need you." She cursed softly, but got up anyway. At the stairs she turned and looked straight at him.

"Maybe you are right, I need my sleep." Turnog nodded and she walked up the stairs, leaving him alone.

TURNOG SIGHED AND LOOKED at the closed outer door, for a moment he considered checking Skegg's. He had probably fallen asleep in the stable. Something he used to do and when he did he didn't want to wake him up. Like Ravana, he had slept Skegg and needed full of energy in their journey to the other realms. He got up and walked to the stairs.

"So you let her live?" He froze and quickly looked around.

"Where are you Isodora?" A single laugh echoed across the room, he straightened his back and folded his arms.

"Show yourself, I want to look into your eyes when I talk to you." He kept staring straight ahead, she appeared right in front of him. He didn't want to reward her by showing her he was shocked, yet a mean smile appeared on her face.

"Here I am and I would like an answer to my question." His eyebrows shot up, she used to make his heart beat faster or even stop. But now he felt nothing but great envy.

"You ask about the known way, so you don't need an answer from me." She smiled and shook his head and put her slender hand on his chest.

"Since when have you been so numb." He turned his hand away and looked her straight into her sea-green eyes.

"I'm not numb, I just don't feel anything for you." She stepped back, startled, but she recovered quickly, perhaps a little too soon.

"You hurt me deeply." He shook his head and just took a step towards her.

"I'm not hurting you, but you're a good actor. Maybe you should leave your witchcraft life behind and build a new one." Isodora turned away from him.

"But you are right and I do have my answer. But notice my words if you do nothing to her, then"

"Then what, then you do it yourself!" She frowned for a moment, then nodded.

"I don't know about you, but I am fed up with this realm and I want to live a normal life again." It was impossible to blow steam from his nose, but if he could, he would have done it.

"I want you to go and you leave Helana alone, if you don't I will kill you." Visibly not suppressed, she laughed off his warning.

"I'm not easy to get scared and certainly not because of you." She pointed her finger at his heart.

"For I am the daughter of the sea and land." It was his turn to laugh, which surprised her. But he wanted her to leave, and he took another step toward her.

"I want you to leave my father's house." Isodora shook her head, clearly she had other plans.

"By my father's name, I command you to leave this house silver fox daughter of the sea." Isodora stamped her left foot hard, like a young child who doesn't get her way. But still disappeared before his eyes and he breathed a sigh of relief.

"YOU DID WELL, CAPTAIN." Skegg walked through the front door, a satisfied smile on his face.

"What are you doing up?" Turnog didn't want to show that he was surprised to see Skegg after evicting Isodora from the house. Skegg shrugged, it just showed that he was an old man. Something he wouldn't normally pay attention to, but when it was so clearly visible he couldn't deny it and it made him all the more concerned about the man's health.

"I couldn't sleep and then I saw that witch. I must admit that I listened to gulls and I can repeat what I said when I just came in." He raised his hand and shook his head.

"Thank you, but now really to bed Skegg. I need you tomorrow and as always the journey to the other realm is getting tougher." Skegg staggered slowly over to him and put a hand on his shoulder.

"There is nothing I cannot handle, Captain. Nothing that can touch me, because I stand here as a proud man." Turnog slowly pushed Skegg's hand away.

"Anything can happen, whether you are proud of me or not. Especially if you don't get enough sleep, so walk." Turnog said it perhaps a little too loudly and he was startled by his tone, it was because of Isodora he quickly shook those thoughts away and looked at Skegg who nodded in agreement.

"As you wish, captain."

FINALLY TURNOG LAY under the sheets himself, staring at the ceiling, but no matter how hard he tried to sleep and rest, he didn't want to find him. The thoughts of leaving Helana to the whims of Isodora kept him wide awake. Even the knowledge that Helana now wore the soul of the sea offered him no rest. Soon, far too quickly, the sun shone through the windows and a rumbling down the hallway from Skegg and Ravana penetrated his bedroom door. There was nothing for it but to get up and get ready for the journey to the other realm.

To wait

Helana

The rumbling came through the wooden bedroom, before long other sounds mixed with the rumbling. Helana trow the sheets away and got up quickly, as quick as she could she dressed herself, she wanted to see them some time before they left. She had been wearing pants when she road horseback, yet it felt strange and so she put on the dress Ravana had given her. For a moment she looked at herself in the mosaic mirror, her cheeks had regained some color. That was a good sign, but she didn't want to dwell on it. Helana lowered her eyes and grabbed her brush, brushing the tangles from her brown hair with long strokes. She shook her hair for a moment, at least that's what her mother always did. She immediately put on the diadeem and then left her room.

IT WAS QUIET DOWNSTAIRS and for a moment she became afraid that the others had already left until she walked into the kitchen. The conversation that took place stopped immediately as soon as she entered.

"Did we wake you up?" Turnog stood up and walked over to her, she shook her head. His hands grabbed her over arms and looked deep into her eyes. But she just gave him a smile and he pulled her close.

"Sorry." She knew why he was apologizing, but she didn't want to remember it. Especially now that he was about to leave her temporarily.

"Come back to me." He pushed her gently away from him and nodded.

"As long as you keep waiting for me." It was her turn to nod, where to go. That they probably had all the answers and all she could do was fight the realm that was slowly killing her. She pushed herself back against him, enjoying the sound of his beating heart.

"Turnog it's time." Ravana's voice was calm, which reassured her. She let go of him and took a few steps back. She looked at others for a moment and they answered with a small nod to the question she had not yet asked.

"Try to keep yourself busy, from experience I know that time goes faster then." Helana lowered her head in a playful way, but she quickly laughed.

"I will do my best." Skegg nodded a moment and then walked out of the room, followed closely by Turnog.

"ISODORA WAS HERE LAST night." Ravana's voice drew her back to the kitchen.

"What?" Ravana nodded in agreement.

"That was my reaction, but the fact that she was here doesn't change." She sighed and clenched her fists, why couldn't that witch leave them alone.

"She used the same trick, but Turnog seemingly refused to talk to her unless he could see her. It worked because Skegg saw her too."

“To be honest, I don't care if she was visible or not. All I want to know is what she did here.”

Ravana folded her arms and nodded in understanding.

"She wanted to know if we let you live or not." Helana swallowed for a moment and her thoughts immediately went free again, this should not get any crazier. She had enough on her mind now that she knew that the only way to survive is if one gave their life for the other. But now she still had to watch out for Isodora or at least that's what she expected.

"As you might expect, she threatened to take matters into her own hands." So Ravana was right.

"Thanks for warning me now that I know." Helana shook her head in disbelief and put a hand on her forehead. But instead of her forehead, touched the cold jewel. "Fortunately I have some form of protection thanks to you, even though it takes some getting used to."

"You shouldn't put too much faith in magical items. But I don't need to tell you that, you're almost an expert in legends." Helana laughed and shook her head, then shrugged.

"Not an expert, but I'm probably getting close. My grandfather was the real expert, but shouldn't you go?" Ravana looked out in alarm and nodded. She wanted to say something else.

"Ravana, are you coming?" Skegg's bored voice echoed throughout the house

"See you later." Ravana gave a quick wave and ran out of the kitchen.

HELANA FINISHED HER breakfast and took Skegg's advice in good spirits. She washed the dishes and washed the bedding. The weather was lovely, so she let the laundry blow in the salty wind, catching herself looking up every time. She waited until she saw the white sails on the horizon, then went back to work with a curse.

THE BEDS WERE MADE again, the whole house smelled of the salty sea breeze. Now Helana faced a problem, she couldn't think of anything more to do. Even the stables were scrubbed clean and the horses also had a good brushing. There was nothing to do but wait and hope it wouldn't be long. She settled into her usual spot on the cliff and let her thoughts wander. The same question came to her again, why couldn't Isodora leave her alone. She had already done enough damage, she had to learn to let go. Maybe it was easy for her to talk, the man she has some kind of relationship with was still there. While Isodora's, but as Turnog said it was an accident. A sigh left her and she narrowed her gaze to stare better into the distance. One seagull swooped past her down and plunged into the surf. Not much later the animal surfaced again with a fish in its beak. She looked at the animal in disbelief, it had no trace of fear. How she would like to trade with the animal, but it was not that easy. It probably took a lot more to quell her fears. Still, she meant what she said yesterday, she would like to give her life. Helana was put to death anyway, and she was sure she wouldn't want to live without him. But she could have guessed that he thought the same way. Why couldn't they both win and build a life together.

THE NEXT THING HELANA felt was a hand shove her. She staggered for a moment to maintain her weight and turned quickly, two sea-green eyes staring at her. Again Isodora pushed her, and this time her feet lost the grip of the solid ground. She tried to surrender to the fall and braced herself for the pain her fall would cause. To her surprise, the pain did not materialize as the sea hugged her. Her dress filled with the water and as much as she fought against it, it pulled her down further and further. Helana had only one option and that was somehow to take the dress off. She knew how long she had before her lungs would scream for oxygen, so she immediately fought the string on her chest that held the dress together. She already struggled with that on land, but now she was also fighting the water that slowed her movements. Helana doesn't know how but the string broke and the grip the dress had on her weakened with some fiddling, and she wrung herself out and swam to the surface as fast as she could.

HELANA IMMEDIATELY gasped as she began treading water to keep her head above water. She circled quickly and looked at the white rock face of the cliff that rose above her. It seemed higher now that she looked up from the bottom, her gaze fell on a figure at the top of the cliff. Most likely Isodora, who disappeared into thin air as quickly as she was used to. But she could not call for further attention there, she had to get into the harbor before the current strengthened under the influence of the full moon.

HELANA CURSED FOR A moment that she'd cleaned the entire house, her muscles begging her to stop what she was doing. Maybe she should, but give in to her fatigue and then she would be rid of it. That saved Turnog the difficult decision and then he was free to move on with his life. Helana didn't know if it was tears or the sea water, she just insisted that the two had mixed together. Since when did she give up so easily, she was a Summernight and they fought for everything they had. But she was so tired and she could no longer, her body could no longer. She bit her lip, she hadn't expected this from herself. It scared her a little. She gasped and started swimming again, wanted to see him again. She didn't want to drown, she wanted to live and for that she had to fight. For a moment she heard her grandfather's voice in her head.

"That'is the spirit, Helana." She wanted to smile, but just to be sure, she didn't.This was really something he would say, without a doubt.

"MAN OVERBOARD!" HELANA immediately stopped swimming when she heard it. She turned and the Steria came her way, someone jumped into the water and she didn't want to be picky but she hoped it was Ravana. Since she was forced to swim in her underwear. The one got closer and closer, and to her relief, it was indeed Ravana.

"What are you doing here?"

"Isodora." Ravana nodded and narrowed her eyes.

"Come on I'll take you to the ship." Helana looked at her anxiously for a moment. "What, what's up?" Helana sighed, Ravana would find out on her own.

"The dress I was wearing was too heavy to swim in." Ravana shrugged, of course she had guessed it long ago. It had been her dress before she lent it.

"Come on, let's go." The two of them swam to the ship, a rope made sure that she was not pulled under the ship. They climbed up on a rope loader, Ravana led the way.

"Skegg a sheet please!"

"Coming." Ravana jumped over the wooden balustrade with great ease.

"Thanks Skegg and now turn around!" A murmur rose from the deck. "I said turn around and don't let any of you see sea rats!"

"You hear her, this is not a question, this is an order." Helana's heart skipped a beat, it was strange just now she was ready to give up and now all that feeling was gone.

"That also applies to you, Captain." There was silence, but Ravana's hand motioned for her to crawl aboard. The sheet was wrapped around her and a relieved sigh left her lungs. She was safe.

Boiling blood

Turnog

Turnog's blood was boiling, when Ravana asked everyone to turn around he thought she was joking. But when she gave the green flame to turn around again he was shocked what he saw. Helana was trembling in the woolen sheet that Skegg had given her. But when she mentioned that Isodora had pushed her off the cliff, he could hardly contain his anger.

"I'll kill that witch." Helana walked up to him and took his arm.

"That is not necessary, am I still alive?" She was right about that, but it could be because of the soul of the sea. Ravana shouted orders to the crew in his stead, for his thoughts were no longer on this ship.

"Come to my cabin, I may have some extra clothes." They walked to his cabin together.

"Why do you have extra clothes with you?" He raised his shoulders.

"My father always had extra clothes with him in case a new crew member came in. Often those poor wretches wore very worn rags and then he offered them a new outfit. That's how he gained their trust and I have taken over that habit." He knelt by a molar and opened it gently. A cloud of dust appeared and a pile of clothing became visible. He reached into the box and took off pants and a T-shirt.

"Pull up here, when we are docked we can look at women's clothing." Turnog handed the pile of clothes to her. Because of his anger, he didn't hear her thank him and he left her.

"WHAT ARE YOU GOING to do when we reach the harbor?" Ravana was waiting for Turnog, folded her arms and looking at him intently.

"I'm going to look for Isodora and end her life, maybe that will break the curse without either of us having to die."

"It doesn't work like that when she dies, this realm just continues to exist with all its conveniences and inconveniences, I'm surprised I have yet to tell you this." There she had a good point, something he forgot because of his anger.

"What would I do without you?"

"You would walk in seven seas at once." Turnog nodded, calming down a bit but the thoughts of killing Isodora still haunted his mind.

"And you wouldn't get any satisfaction from it." He stepped aside so Helana could join them.

"I disagree, I would get quite a lot of satisfaction out of it and I warned her. So if I don't do it, I come across as weak." Helana folded her arms, the T-shirt he'd given her was way too big for her. But she could take it anyway, he shook off those thoughts.

"By whom are you seen as weak, by us or by Isodora." Helana quickly exchanged glances with Ravana who nodded in agreement, this he again had two women who had shared their strengths.

"CAPTAIN, HARBOR IN sight" That was his salvation, Turnog apologized and wanted to run. But Ravana grabbed his arm.

"I'll go, you talk on." Before he could argue, she had already left. Turnog took a deep breath and turned his attention back to Helana. Still looking at him intently with her intelligent blue eyes, he immediately knew he was lost. But what else could he do, he was a man of his word and he had warned Isodora.

"I know what you're thinking, but I won't let you go. She's done enough to hurt you, don't let her take your humanity away too." Turnog took a few steps back, he hadn't looked at it that way yet.

"But what else can I do, pretend she just didn't push you off the cliff." Helana nodded and dropped her arms.

"If that calms you down, then yes. Pretend I wasn't pushed off that cliff." She looked so tired, swimming had exhausted her.

"If want me to do that, I'll do it for you." She shook her head.

"Do it for you and not for me. It's your humanity, or what's left of what's at stake. Your men won't look at you any differently." Turnog turned and the men closest to them had their ears open to the conversation, a few nodded in agreement at Helana's words.

"What do you think you are doing, get to work!" He couldn't help showing that he was still in charge of this ship, even though he was being lectured by a woman in men's clothing. Something he was used to, he grew up with Ravana. But Helana was a stranger to him and yet she wanted to save him from future mistake. When he looked at her again she had narrowed her eyes, he had not yet given her what she wanted and she was waiting for that now.

"There is no other option than to agree with you. But I can't forgive the witch for what she wanted to do to you."

"She wanted to do it, but she didn't succeed and that's the most important thing." He nodded in agreement, but his fists were clenched.

TURNOG BREATHED A SIGH of relief when they returned to the lighthouse. Skegg looked approvingly at the clean-polished wood, everything smelled cleaner than when they left that morning, too.

"Princess, you have been busy." Something he could only agree to, Skegg stretched.

"Then I'll go, but clean out the horse stables."

"I've already done that, you just have to feed them." Skegg's jaw dropped, Ravana looked at her in disbelief.

"What did you do?" Helana began to list everything. "Have we really been gone that long?"

Helana nodded a moment, then shrugged.

"I didn't mind doing it and it was badly needed, it wasn't an insult to you Skegg." Turnog shrugged and walked out of the house to the stable to feed the horses. Turnog walked over to her and put a hand on her shoulder.

"Thank you." Turnog couldn't say more about it, he was impressed by the work she had done. Helana shrugged again.

"What should I have done differently?" It was a good question, of course, but she wouldn't have had to clean the entire house, including the stables. She suppressed a yawn behind the back of her hand. Ravana saw it too and went straight to the kitchen, stopped in the doorway.

"I'll make something to eat." Ravana pointed to Helana. "You sit down, you have done enough." Turnog pushed back the nearest chair and pushed Helana onto the chair with a single hand.

"I'll watch her." Turnog looked at Ravana, who nodded and disappeared into the kitchen.

TURNOG PUT THE SOMETHING in his mouth, he couldn't say what it was or what it tasted like. For a moment he looked at Ravana who now also looked at him, she probably had the same problem.

"Is something wrong?" He closed his eyes for a moment and sighed.

"Every time we sail out and come back, this realm takes something away from us and this time it was our sense of taste." Helana looked at him in disbelief.

"Why does the realm do that, he already feeds on my life energy." He could shrug, he had no answer for that question.

"You eat quietly and then go to bed with you." She shook her head for a moment, but suppressed another yawn. "Before you say you're not tired, I'll figure you out." Her cheeks burned a little with shame, but he didn't care. When she suppressed another yawn, he hit the table with a flat hand. "Okay, to bed with you." Turnog saw that she wanted to fight again, but he shook his head. She dropped her head with a sigh and got up slowly. As soon as he heard her bedroom door slam, he got up.

"I'll be right back." Ravana also got up and ran to the door, blocking his way out.

"No, I know what you are going to do and I will not let you go."

Harsh words

Ravana

Turnog sighed and that made Ravana's blood boil, he thought she didn't notice. Since when did he have such a low impression of her.

"I have to go, it's something I have to do." Ravana shook her head and spread her arms so that she looked a little taller.

"No, you don't have to do anything at all. Helana was right. Isodora has taken enough from us and I don't like her taking any more." He raised his hand, which he always did when he wanted to silence someone. He needed to know that it didn't work for her, she turned her hand away. "You are still my younger brother and I listen to you if I want to, but now you listen to me." He grabbed her.

"I won't hurt her, I'm just going there to talk. I'm a man of my word and I know you won't see me any differently if I don't, but I have to do this for myself." She shook her head again.

"No, I won't let you go yet." Turnog let go of her and folded his arms.

"Do not you trust me?" She shook her head for the thirth time.

"It's not that I don't trust you, I don't trust her."

RAVANA WAS AWAKENED by the door slamming shut, that was strange the sun hadn't even risen, even though it wasn't long before. For a moment she tried to remember if anyone had suggested an early job the night before. But all that came up was that Turnog wanted to go to Isodora to talk. She had blocked his way, she gasped. She threw off the sheets and ran to his bedroom. The bed had not been slept in, she cursed. She knew where he had gone, and she could no longer protect him from possible mistakes he might make. When he was angry, he was capable of anything.

"Ravana?" Ravana turned, Helana standing in her own bedroom doorway. She cursed again, she hadn't meant to wake Helana.

"Sorry, Helana. Did I wake you up?" Helana shook her head.

"I was already awake, but when I heard you, I got up." Ravana sighed with relief, because that was something she couldn't take with it. Helana tilted her head slightly.

"He went to her, didn't he?" Startled, she looked at the young woman, who clearly understood what was going on. Reluctantly she nodded and swore again.

"How could I be so stupid as to believe he was going to sleep." Helana came out of her doorway and took her arm.

"It's not your fault." Ravana said nothing more, but burst into her own room, slamming the door shut. Ravana looked in amazement at the now closed door, but not much later Helana came out again. She was wearing her rider's outfit and walked past her to the stairs.

"Where are you going?" Ravana ran after her, down the stairs.

"What does it look like, I'm going after him." Ravana sighed.

"You two are a two peas in a bucket, a pot is too small." Helana turned her head, her eyes flashing.

"Do you have a better idea?" Ravana froze like she had never seen Helana before. But on the other hand, she had only known her for a month.

"No, but I'm sure he won't walk in seven seas at the same time." Helana turned back and walked to the front door.

"Not on purpose no, but I want to be there just in case." Ravana couldn't deny that she didn't want the same and sighed.

"Wait a minute and then I'll put on pants and go with you." She ran upstairs as fast as she could and jumped into pants. She was about to leave her room when she heard horse hooves running away, she ran downstairs, being careful not to fall down the stairs in her haste. "You see, they are exactly the same."

Storm on the way

Helana

Helana couldn't wait any longer, confident that Turnog would keep his word. But she had her doubts about Isodora. She had saddled the horse as fast as she could and was riding away from the lighthouse, the road was hard to see. The full moon, which should have given enough light, was displaced by thick storm clouds and a violent gust of wind blew over the island. She clung to the animal that seemed to be flying with her knees. Probably if she hadn't been in a hurry, she would have found this very scary, but she didn't want to dwell on her own fears this time.

THE SOUND OF THE HORSES' hooves she heard a few days earlier as she rode across the stone bridge was carried away by the wind, and in the darkness the trees in the forest around it seemed to come to life. A shiver made its way down her bare arms and she cursed herself for not dressing herself warmer. But thinking back to it, she didn't have time to wait for Ravana, and now there was no turning back. Leaving the forest behind, she drove between the steep slopes of the mountains, the violent creaking of the forest died down and gave way to a deafening silence. Something that got on her nerves even more, she knew from last time that quite a few stones were released and could imagine that during a storm like this they could cause an avalanche. Fortunately, the light gray mare was not bothered by this and drove on without stopping.

YET ONLY BREATHED A sigh of relief when she drove into the deserted village, the mountains with the loose stones were far behind them. Helana held the animal in a little, so that it got a little bit of rest, the witch's tower loomed from the darkness. Thanks to the white rock it seemed to glow, which grew stronger the closer she got. Shivers ran down her body again, only they weren't from the cold. At the tower she jumped out of the saddle, she threw the reins over the animal's head. This way she could get away quickly if necessary and with Isodora that was quite a good opportunity. Even the horse was so Turnog at the door, she walked cautiously to the animal, so it's not her could scare. As soon as he saw her, the animal put its ears back tightly.

"Calm down." The ears popped out again when she heard her voice, seemingly a little frightened by the storm. Her grandfather used to let go of the horses when it stormed, so that the animals were free to find their own way. When she saw Turnog's horse, she immediately understood why.

"You don't want to be here at all, wait a little longer, I'll get your owner." The animal shook its head, the sound of the metal bumping into each other was faintly audible in the wind. Not wanting to frighten the animal more than it already was, she sneaked to the door that was ajar, probably not properly closed by Turnog. Or left open on purpose by Isodora who probably suspected that she or Ravana would come after him and therefore made it easier for them to enter without having to interrupt Turnog. Helana hesitated for a moment when she put her hand on the door, but then she pulled the door open anyway and walked in.

Lost

Turnog

Turnog slowly threw the reins over his brown mare 's head, the wind was picking up. Black dark clouds were already gathering before the full moon, this would make it more difficult to get back but he wasn't worried about that just yet. He patted the animal's neck gently, then walked to the large door, already raising his fist to ram it. To his horror, the door flew open, Isodora standing in a short, thin dusty dress in the doorway.

"Hello, dragon of the sea." One of the thin straps fell off her shoulder, revealing part of her bosom for a moment.

"By the grace of my mother, it looks like it's going to be a storm." Isodora looked past him and then back at him. "Where are my manners, come in." Isodora stepped aside and disappeared into the tower. Turnog shook his head in disbelief, it was so obvious he was falling into a trap, he just wasn't sure if the trap was for him or was he just the bait. Against his better judgment, he entered the tower and she closed the door behind him. She walked past him, a scent of rose perfume hung around her. So she was already expecting him. "My compliments on the use of the soul of the sea, it has done its job very well if I say so myself." For a moment he was back on the ship and had just turned around, trying with great pain and effort to control his emotions."But my mom is not known for half work, just look at me." Again the strap had fallen off her shoulder and, for the sake of convenience, he tried not to look at her. She was playing him, so he was the bait.

"I'm here to say that you played well today, you hit. But I get some pleasure out of it that you failed." He gasped for a moment, she was now very close to him.

"What makes you think I failed." Her face was very close to his now, he raised his hands and put them on her shoulders, pushing her away from him. She started to laugh and pulled her straps up from her dress. "You are here now and your sister or Helana, maybe both have probably followed you closely." He folded his arms and sighed.

"So you were planning this when you threatened Helana yesterday?" She nodded and spread her arms. "What do you win with this?" He took a step back, he wanted to understand her. She laughed again.

"What do I gain with this? Isn't that clear?" Turnog shook his head, and she walked forward again and pressed herself against him. "I break that child's heart and you will be blamed for it." Turnog pushed her away again.

"DO YOU REALLY THINK that will work?" Isodora nodded to something behind him, he didn't really want to know who was behind him. He made a small prayer to ask for Ravana. He turned slowly.

"Helana?"Helana immediately approached, her eyes flashing. Fortunately not to him but to Isodora.

"Did you really think I would blame him?" Isodora folded her arms and shook her head from side to side.

"Listen, honey. What you think the two of you have simply doesn't exist." He walked to Helana and then looked at Isodora with disdain.

"What you mean to say you don't know. That doesn't mean it doesn't exist!" Helana stepped forward. Isodora shook her head and rocked her head back and forth again.

"Love is a fairytale, nothing more nothing less. Turnog knows that I am right." Turnog frowned for a moment, that is indeed what he had said to her. But that was at the very beginning.

"Even for you it is low to use someone's words against them." Isodora looked at him in disbelief and he sighed. "That's how I thought about it."

"But let me guess, it's different with her. Please." Helana took a few steps away from him. He walked over to her but she walked to the door.

"Helana, please." But she shook her head.

"Isodora is right, you are going to break my heart." Helana ran out of the tower, he looked briefly at Isodora who started to laugh out loud. He shook his head and ran after Helana.

"You see I win."

Get some fresh air

Helana

Helana sat smiling on her light gray mare, Turnog slammed the door behind him and shook his head in disbelief.

"I thought you meant it." Helana clung to the saddle.

"I just hope she believes it." He threw the reins back over his horse's head.

"I don't know, but if we stay here any longer." She sent the animal to the deserted village.

"Then let's go." Having blessed that, she spurred her horse on and rode off.

"WHERE THE RUSH, WE can now take it a bit easier." Turnog was riding next to her now, they were at the beginning of the valley. Helana glanced up quickly, the sound of the wind hitting the cliffs.

"Let's get over the stone bridge and then we can take it easier." She had to scream to get over the sound of the wind. His gaze also went to the rocks, thanks to the darkness he had not seen the loose stones. The first drop of rain fell on her bare arms, which could be added. Several drops started to fall, which also made the rock walls wet and slippery.

A flash of lightning lit their path, their eyes catching each other. They said nothing but they knew they had to get out of here. Both spurred their animals on, another flash of lightning lit their path for a moment. It was long enough to see a single pebble fall from the cliff face. The sound of the wind was pushed into the background by the sound of the falling rocks. She didn't want to kick the animal too hard, but she couldn't help it.

"What did you say about taking it easy?" Helana looked aside and he shook his head. "Watch out" Her horse jumped away from the rock just in time.

"That was too close to be fun." Helana looked at him and exhaled, all he could do was nod in agreement.

"Maybe it is better to let the horses go." Before he nodded.

"Let's be out of this valley then." Fortunately that was only a short distance, yet she only breathed a sigh of relief when they had left the avalanche valley. "It seems safe enough here." Helana restrained her horse, he did the same, but looked around just to be sure.

"Are you sure this is a good idea?" Helana shook her head, but then dismounted.

"But my grandfather let the horses go in a storm." He sighed and dismounted too, knotting the reins together so tightly. "Why do you do that?" He didn't look at her as he tied the stirrups to the saddle.

"They can get stuck by their reins and stirrups. By tying them tightly against the horse we prevent that." It made sense, she had never heard of her grandfather about it, but he may never have needed this method. She started tying the reins and stirrups.

"Are you ready?" She nodded and stepped away from her horse.

"Ready." The horses ran side by side into the forest, she sighed.

"NOW WE HAVE TO WALK the rest." Helana clenched her fists and gave him a playful punch in the arm.

"What does that make you think." They walked side by side into the forest, the wind roughly playing with branches. Every so often she watched the branches sway dangerously back and forth.

"Don't worry, it's no more dangerous here than in the valley." Helana hit him on the arm again.

"Ouch!" He rubbed the spot where she hit him. "You hit hard, for a girl." Their eyes widened and gasped, but she didn't hit him again. She set her foot on the stone bridge, a deafening creak muffled the sound of the wind again. She turned to see a tree striking his side, ran to him and pushed him aside. She herself also jumped away from the tree, but slipped.

THE COLD WATER OF THE river stung her skin, the current took her with it.

"Helana!" Helana heard him call before she submerged.

Against the current

Turnog

Turnog scanned the surface of the water, Helana just couldn't come up. He cursed and stood on the edge of the stone bridge.

"What are you going to do, she can't drown." Once again a curse left his mouth, she couldn't for once not poke her nose into his business.

"Let me be, Isodora." Turnog didn't even look at her, she was nothing more to him than a faint voice in the wind.

"Don't let me stop you." It was he not going and he jumped into the cold water. Immediately the current took possession of him and took him away, trying to keep his head above water and at the same time to search for Helana.

"Helana!" His mouth filled with water, he quickly spat the water out. "Helana!" He didn't got an answer, he slowly swam with the current.

TURNOG HAD ARRIVED at the gigantic lake where the water normally stayed for a while before continuing its way to the sea. But the river forget that the lake was there and immediately made his way to the sea. He had hoped he'd already found her, he called her name again.

"Turnog!" He looked quickly at where the noise was coming from, a little further up a tree had fallen and ended up partly in the river. She had clung to one of the outstretched branches. He swam to the tree, crashed into a branch. However, the water had other plans and tried to pull him along again, with great difficulty he grabbed one of the branches and let the water pull on his body.

"Turnog!" Helana hung a little farther from him, her branch a bit thicker than his.

"I'm here. Are you okay?" Helana nodded slowly, fear was still written in her eyes. He had to distract her, something that would make them forget their approached situation for a moment. "Hey, do you come here more often?" If he didn't have to hold the branch he could hit himself in the head, what was the point. But against his expectations a smile appeared on her face and for a little For a moment the fear had disappeared from her eyes.

TURNOG HEARD A CRACK, he quickly glanced at his branch but as far as he could see it was still intact and showed no cracks.

"Did you hear that too?" Something cracked again, his gaze moved to her branch. That, that moment broke. Immediately she was dragged back into the water again, without thinking about it he let go of his branch. The current took possession of him, everything in him told him to fight it but he ignored it and swam to her as best he could.

"I have got you." Turnog grabbed her hand and pulled her toward him with great difficulty until she was completely glued to him. He looked around for a moment, he recognized this place they were now close to the mouth to the sea. In the water he tried to turn the two of them over.

"What are you doing?" Helana clung to his with all her body.

"We are almost at the sea." She looked up and a trace of recognition sparkled in her eyes.

"The rocks." She said it almost silently, but she seemed to be screaming in his ears. She kept looking into his eyes, his heart stopped beating. For a moment she looked up, her eyes widened and a dull thump could be heard. A cutting pain echoed through his body, the sound of creaking bones filling his ears. He looked into her eyes for a moment before slipping her out of his grip, he wanted to reach for her again but his body refused to respond. His vision slowly clouded before everything in his world turned black.

The curse has been broken

Helana

Helana woke up slowly, slowly she got up. Her whole body was shaking, not from the rain still falling, but from what. She couldn't remember, she turned so she could sit on the wet white beach. She looked out over the stormy sea, how did she get here. She blinked a few times, slowly the memories returned to her. She looked around quickly, where was Turnog. She scrambled to her feet and staggered to her feet.

"Turnog!" Her voice was weak and shaky. She took a deep breath and tried again.

"Helana!" It was not Turnog's voice, but Ravana's voice. Her heart stopped when lightning struck the sea, she had seen that before, but then the lightning didn't have a sea green color.

"No," Ravana was standing next to her now, and sorrow echoed in her voice. She too felt tears well in her eyes.

"Tell me it isn't." They looked at each other and she thought the same thing, yet her tears told them that they had both lost hope that it was not true.

"Princess, Ravana." Skegg and the other crew came running. Their clothes stuck to their bodies. Skegg came to a stop in front of them and leaned forward to catch his breath. "We just came out of the tavern and saw the lightning, where is the captain?" He looked around in surprise, his eyes looking for Turnog.

"We do not know." He looked at her in surprise.

"What do you mean, you don't know. Weren't you with him?" This was the first time she had heard Skegg talk like that, she looked quickly at Ravana who also looked at Skegg in amazement.

"Skegg, it's not her fault. The storm the losses to another awful and there are multiple ways."

Skegg lowered his head and sighed, as he raised his head, tears ran down his cheeks.

"I know that too. But I had to promise your father that if anything should happen to him. That I had to look after you and I take that promise seriously." Ravana walked over to him and put a hand on his arm.

"I know that." He looked at her and hung his head again.

ONCE AGAIN A SEA-GREEN lightning shot through the sky and the clouds burst from one.

"The curse is broken." The murmur came from one of the crew, she could only nod. "But that means," Helana raised her hands and pressed them to her ears, not wanting to hear the rest of the sentence. This would only confirm what she already knows, it shouldn't have been that way they had another month until she gave her own life for him. She was dying anyway and that would shorten her agony, but that time has now been stolen from them. A hand was placed on her shoulder, she didn't have to look at the person to know it was Skegg. She dropped her hands from her ears.

"Ravana is right, it's not your fault." She threw herself against him and broke, he could have pushed her away. But he just put his arms around her. "I know you wanted to give your own life to save ours." His voice was soft and almost inaudible. She looked up and was startled, his face was made of sand. She took a quick step back, his arms broke apart and the whole shape of his body fell apart.

"What is happening." Helana watched the other crew members fall apart one by one. Their bodies mixed with the sand.

"So Skegg was right after all." Ravana's voice, too, was nothing more than a whisper in the wind. Something that caused a lot of concern.

"What was he right about?" Helana walked over to Ravana and she opened her mouth to answer, but fell apart before she could do it.

Silence after the storm

Helana

Helana stared at the sea, she had seen the sun rise slowly. She couldn't bring herself to move, she had now lost not only Turnog but Ravana and Skegg as well. She had no more tears to cry on and let the salty wind play with her hair. The screams of the awakening gulls were her only companions besides the calm waves. Until the beach was filled with children playing. She was not bothered by that and kept staring straight ahead.

"HELANA?" HELANA HEARD a voice she never expected to hear. "Is it really you?" She turned to Suzania's voice, the woman covering her mouth with her hand. Tears streamed down her cheeks, one two-year-old boy was holding her other hand. A man also walked up and she recognized him as Harbor Master Treuman. Which came to a stop next to Suzania.

"At Aqray in the sky and Tishilla in the sea. Helana!" He ran to her and lifted her up. She let out a little cry of shock, startled him and put her gently on the ground. "It's really you."

She nodded slowly and collapsed. He caught her just in time before she hit the sand. "I'll take her home and you go get a doctor." He had turned his attention to Suzania who had been watching her frozen, but as soon as Helana looked at her she thawed and knelt down by the child.

"Skegg, stay with your father."The boy nodded and she ran away.

HELANA WAS CARRIED into the lighthouse house, her gaze immediately turned to the portrait of Turnog. She would ask Treuman if he could hang it in her room once everything was back to normal, if that was still possible. In their eyes she had come back from the dead, and that she thought about it like that, they were not far off. She was put on the bed.

"Daddy, who is that lady?" Treuman turned to the child, pushed herself a little bit and beckoned the child. Who walked carefully to her.

"Sorry where are manners. I haven't introduced myself yet, my name is Helana Summernight and who are you?"

"Skegg Treuman, Mrs. Summernight." She gave him a big smile.

"Nice to meet you Skegg Treuman." The doctor came in together with an agent, the doctor asked for the usual such as name and date of birth. After she answered everything, he examined her thoroughly.

"You're just exhausted, not crazy for someone who has been pronounced dead for two years." Startled, she looked at the doctor, then at the others in the room. Treuman was the only one to nod in agreement.

"Sorry did you say two years?" The doctor just nodded.

"The last thing we heard is that you and your parents left on the Jewel of the sea." Helana looked at the cop who had spoken and now sat up straight.

"And now you want to know where I've been all this time." The officer folded his arms and nodded.

"That seems logical to me, people don't normally come back from death." She wanted to argue with him but changed her mind quickly. "Nor do you seem to have aged a day than when you left." She sighed.

"To be honest officer, you wouldn't believe me if I told you. I don't believe it anymore and I've been there." The officer laughed.

"I grew up here so the line of what I believe and what not is very thin." She shrugged, she had warned him, and she started telling.

FROM THE MOMENT THEY left the harbor here, until the moment Ravana fell apart on the beach. His mouths had fallen open in surprise, and the officer eyes had a glimmer of disbelief. She had expected he wouldn't believe her.

"That's a really wonderful story, Mrs. Summernight and let's just say for a moment that I believe you. I don't think the rest of the world is that willing." She shrugged her shoulders.

"But officer, we live in a strange world."

THE DOCTOR AND THE officer had left the house, Treuman and Skegg had also left the room.

"How glad I am that you are back home." Suzania sat on the bed.

"But is everything you told the officer really true?" Helana could only nod, tears stung her eyes and she sighed.

"Sorry." Suzania shook her head.

"It's not your fault, your father was forewarned." Helana looked steadily at the woman on the bed, her father was not to blame either.

No, the fault lay with Isodora who could not control her anger, who could not resist playing with other people's feelings. No her father was a victim in Isodora's web.

"I better go to sleep. I probably have to fight to take control of my father's company and I need all my energy for that." Suzania nodded and left the room.

HELANA HAD BEEN RIGHT, it was really a struggle to get the company under her control. It was over a year before they finally could sit quietly in her father's office, she flipped through some paperwork when entered her assistant.

"Mrs. Summernight, your carriage is ready." Amazed, Helana looked up, why was her carriage in front. "The statue of the Steria crew will be unveiled today in Truport and you immediately wanted to stick to it for a weekend." Her assistant gave her a smile and she sighed.

"Thanks, Aqauta. I had completely forgotten about it because of all the hustle and bustle."

Helana grabbed her coat bag and put the papers she just flipped through.

"See you after the weekend, Mrs. Summernight." Helana nodded politely as she walked past, her assistant who reminded her of Isodora, and she would do something to that after the weekend.

HELANA STOOD ON A PLATFORM, in front of her almost all the inhabitants of Truport were waiting patiently.

" Dear Truport residents, my friends. Thank you for coming here, before Captain Summernight's widow and her children found a place in this harbor town it was a pirate's nest. I don't know what it was like before the dragon of the sea took control about the city, but I know he made sure everyone was welcome. It was his sworn oath that he and his crew would protect the inhabitants from gangs and other dangers. For too long we have ignored this piece of history and there we are now all putting an end to it. " Helana took the scissors and walked to the sea-green ribbon, she cut the ribbon in one smooth motion. "Residents of Truport, here I give you the last crew of the Steria, soul of the sea." The cloth covering the image slipped off. The copper statue became visible. The statue of Turnog looked straight ahead to the sea, Ravana and Skegg stood by his side. Ravana with the gutter in her hands and Skegg with his arms folded and a big smile on his face. Applause arose, she turned to the crowd and stepped aside.

SHE STOOD ON THE CLIFF, inhaling the salty air, the statue's likeness to her memories were shockingly the same. Not that she expected otherwise, she had given the sculptor very clear directions and he had been able to study Turnog's portrait well.

"It looks like him." She swore.

"I thought I was delivered from you." A chuckle arose and Isodora came to stand next to her.

"Come on you won't get rid of me that easy. But my time will come just like yours." Helana sighed as her hand went to the chain around her neck. The soul of the sea hung from the chain.

"I actually hoped your time had come when the other one turned to sand before my very eyes" Isodora shrugged, she could turn off the smile on the witch's face. "I miss them every day of my life and I owe that lack to you." Isodora nodded in agreement and looked at the sea.

"You are right about that and somewhere deep in my heart I miss them too." Helana wasn't sure whether to believe the witch. "I understand if you don't believe me." It was Helana's turn to shrug.

"I have to go back to work, goodbye Isodora." Isodora grabbed her arm.

"Not so fast, princess." Helana turned, a gutter hanging from her belt. She had found the weapon in the attic of the house.

"Let go of me silver fox. I'm done with your and your magic." Isodora shook her head.

"Then why do you still have the soul of the sea around your chicken neck?" Helana tore her arm free from Isodora's grip.

"I don't have to explain myself to you and now I'm saying it for the last time. Leave me alone!" Helana wanted to run away again, and again Isodora took her arm. Helana grabbed the gutter from her belt and punched it in Isodora's chest, hearing the witch breathe.

"We warned you." Helana pulled the gutter out of the chest and gave her a hard shove. Isodora fell off the cliff and disappeared into the waves with a dull splash.

HELANA LOOKED OUT TO sea and on the horizon she saw a familiar ship with white sails sailing away. For a moment she turned her attention to the flag, which bore the symbol of the dragon of the sea.

"We will see each other again." The words were carried on the wind and the ship disappeared in a sea-green flash.

Also by Nathalia Books

A Thicket of Thorns story
Book of Secrets

Nathalia's Shorts
Unexpected
Written in the Sand

Nova Babylon
Nova Babylon

Standalone
The Steria

Watch for more at https://nathalia-books-1993.webnode.nl/.

About the Author

Nathalia Books is a real dreamer and turns these dreams into stories. Each with their own world and charm, she prefers to write all day long, and she loves to forget the world around her. Her worlds take you to deserted places and new unknown cities. She introduces you to new unknown races and beliefs.

Read more at https://nathalia-books-1993.webnode.nl/.

About the Publisher

Natalia's publishing is the name Nathalia Books gives to her indy work. Working at a kitchen table with a good cup of coffee, the books come together,

CPSIA information can be obtained
at www.ICGtesting.com
Printed in the USA
LVHW040017280921
698843LV00002B/92